BLUE SKIES DREAMING

TRINITY LAKES ROMANCE BOOK ELEVEN

AMANDA DEED

Visit Amanda Deed at www.amandadeed.com.

© Amanda Deed 2024

Blue Skies Dreaming A Trinity Lakes Romance

Published by Free inDeed Media, 2024

www.freeindeedmedia.com

FREE inDEED MEDiA

ISBN 978-0-6458404-2-1 (e-book)

ISBN 978-0-6458404-3-8 (paperback)

Cover design by Annie Millard

Layout by Carolyn Miller

Edited by Christian Editing Services

In memory of Don and Nathan Green, two men who stood out among a thousand. You are greatly loved and missed. May you rest in the arms of Jesus.

CHAPTER ONE

"What is this, an intervention?"

Violet Reynolds laughed uneasily as she eyed her friends. They had gathered at her house, rather her father's house, on the hill in the Country Club Estate. Nothing unusual there. They often met together to catch up, and her place was the easiest—perhaps roomiest—to hang out in. Okay, so it also had the best views of the mountains and down over the lakes.

Amelia, her long-time assistant and now dear friend, chewed her lip. A dead giveaway. But Amelia averted her gaze to the table of canapes and did not respond. Yes, something fishy was going on.

"Come on, Vi." Breanna's tone was almost scolding. "You haven't been yourself since Australia."

And thank you for the reminder. What a debacle that was. Breanna had a point, though. Fresh out of college and straight into her role of evaluating tour companies for her father, Violet had made one stupid mistake after another, and Daddy was still disappointed in her. He'd always said her impulsiveness would get her into trouble. And he was right. Twice in one trip. That was enough to make anyone doubt themselves.

But lately she'd learned that placing her trust in Jesus, not in herself or in her father, was a better way to go. She was growing stronger by the day. She should tell her friends about her newfound faith and opened her mouth to do so, but then the words stuck in her throat. What if they laughed at her? Didn't believe her?

Besides, she also had the debonair Alistair Harrington paying her attention. Not that her friends knew about that either—it was too soon to make any kind of declaration. Especially when the media and social sites had an eye on her all the time. But if all that didn't boost one's self-assurance, Violet didn't know what would.

"I'm fine." Violet drew the word out. "I'm just being extra cautious now."

"Cautious?" Lilly this time. "You've done nothing that looks even remotely crazy for almost a year."

"With good reason." It was all she could do not to roll her eyes at them. Instead, she shook herself. "I'm conclusively cured of crazy."

"How do we solve a problem like Vi-o-let?" was Mom's sing-song response every time Violet expressed a spontaneous thought. Daddy took it one step further with his go-to slogan, "Whatever is in your head, do the opposite." They'd labeled her a flibbertigibbet from childhood, doing everything they could to train her out of it. But it wasn't until Australia that the remedy took root.

"No, no, no, no, no." Bree shook her head with a frown. "We can't have that. You've lost confidence in yourself. That's all."

"And we have an idea to help you fix it," Lilly added.

Violet selected a mini toast with smoked salmon and popped it in her mouth to avoid having to respond, glaring at them one by one instead. What were they up to? It couldn't be good. Yes, her confidence had been rattled, but was it that big a deal? Had it been that obvious?

Amelia reached a hand across and squeezed hers. "Vi. You know I wouldn't say anything if I didn't agree." Her eyes were full of compassion. "But I think you need this. I think you should hear them out."

Vi looked at the ceiling. She couldn't win. Daddy wanted her to be polished and moderate, but her friends wanted her to be spontaneous and unreserved. Who was she supposed to be? What did God want her to do? She had no idea. She was still too new to this God thing.

"All right. Let's hear it." Listening didn't mean doing.

Bree moved to the edge of the sofa and leaned forward, clearly eager for whatever plan she had concocted in that blonde head of hers. "Skydiving."

One word. "That's it? You want me to jump out of a moving plane, ten thousand feet in the air?"

The idea thrilled her. Some kind of visceral impulse took hold of her heart and mind. Imagine the sensation of soaring through the air. But no. She wasn't impulsive anymore. She would keep her feet firmly on the ground, thank you very much.

"Yes, Vi. It would be good for you. They say it helps you believe in yourself, prove to yourself how brave you are." Lilly's eyes were wide and genuine.

"I can believe in myself with my feet on the ground." Except she didn't. Believing in God was her only firm footing.

"It would boost your confidence." Bree again.

"I don't need a boost." Even though her heart screamed the opposite.

Silence reigned in the room for a moment. Vi leaned back into the leather sofa while the other girls picked at the food and sipped their sparkling mineral waters.

Amelia cleared her throat. "What if you could fundraise money while skydiving?"

Raising funds for a worthy cause might get her back in Daddy's good books.

Violet turned to Amelia with a scowl. This girl knew how to drive the nails into the coffin. Push the buttons that would make it hard for Violet to refuse. "You drive a hard bargain, Amelia."

"Ha, ha." Bree clapped in victory. "So we—"

"I didn't say yes to anything."

"But you will when you hear this." Bree laughed. "You get other celebrities involved and catch it all on camera."

Another knife twist. These women were pulling out all the ammunition. More celebrities would mean more funds raised. Even better.

Violet ran her palms along her thighs. The temptation was too great, and ideas were exploding in her head. Nothing could go wrong with this event, could it? Apart from parachutes failing and broken bones and death. She laughed internally. That would be a tiny chance. Negligible. Surely.

"All right, if we're doing this, we're going to do it properly."

The three of them jumped up and cheered. Lilly even did a little song and dance. "Vi's going skydiving."

Amelia sat down again. "Wait. What do you mean by properly?"

Violet took a deep breath. "We're not just doing a tandem jump. We're going to do a group formation dive."

"Yesss. This will be awesome." Bree threw up her hands.

Violet picked up her phone. "I should check with Daddy and Mom."

Lilly snatched the phone away before she could even unlock the screen. "No, you don't. You are doing this for yourself. You don't need their permission."

Violet narrowed her eyes at her friends. "You are truly wicked women." A gurgle of laughter bubbled up. They were genuinely trying to help, and she couldn't be cross with them.

"Um …" Amelia looked up from her tablet and raised a hand as if she were in school. Nothing unusual there. She was always googling something. "I've done some quick research. It says you need at least twenty-five jumps under your belt before you can solo dive, let alone dive in formation."

Violet grinned at her. "All right then. You'd better book me in straight away. This is going to be a summer-long project. I should be able to fit in a few days per week, since I'm not travelling. And get onto my contacts who have a large following. See who you can get on board."

"Yes, ma'am." Amelia giggled with a salute.

"That only leaves one question." She eyeballed each of them, endeavoring to keep a straight face. "Which of you is doing the first jump with me?"

A round of awkward clearings of throats and averted gazes met her. Just as she thought. They were all scaredy-cats.

"Bree. I elect you. You've been the loudest and most insistent." She eyed her friend with a challenge.

"Uh-uh." Bree shook her head. "I'm not going up there."

Violet let out a mock sigh. "Then I guess I'm not going either."

Lilly and Amelia laughed, but Bree frowned at her. "That's not fair."

"Completely fair, actually. Are you in, or do we cancel the whole thing right now?"

"Fine." Bree folded her arms and rolled her eyes to the ceiling. "But you'd better not laugh at me if I scream."

Violet placed a hand over her heart and feigned innocence. "Would I do such a thing?" She turned to Amelia. "See if you can book the both of us in for this Saturday, then, all right?"

"Will do." Amelia was already tapping away on her tablet.

"Find out if I need any special equipment or clothing, if I'm going to be doing this regularly."

"Sure. I'll look into it."

Violet scanned her friends' faces. "Are you all happy now?" Happy for her to risk her father's displeasure again? But the idea of skydiving excited her. And it would be a good way to pass her spare time while Daddy decided where he would send her next. Perhaps he wouldn't mind so much. Especially when she brought in thousands of dollars for a worthy cause. She just needed to figure out what cause.

———

Nick Gordon sat at the Franklins' dining table with paperwork spread out in front of him.

"All set, Nick?" Peter came in from the kitchen, hot coffees in hand, and put a mug down beside him.

"I think so." Nick rubbed his face. He could use a break. Reading regulations for so long made his head fuzzy. "It doesn't seem much different from how we run things in Australia." He put down his pen and stretched his arms above his head.

"That's good." Peter pulled out a chair on the opposite side of the table.

"Yeah. Thanks for the coffee. And again, thanks for having me. I really appreciate it."

"No need. You're doing me a big favor by looking after the grounds while you're here."

It had been a week, and Nick had finally got past the jet lag and settled into the opposite time zone from Australia. Finally been able to get his head around the documents for his American summer job and watch an online video instructional. Finally been awake and alert enough for Peter Franklin to show him around the Bible College grounds, the garden shed, where the ride-on mower lived plus any other gardening tools he might need.

The Franklins had offered him room and board in exchange for maintaining the grounds for the summer. And they were great people to be around. He couldn't deny that he'd landed on his feet.

"Do you mind if I ask you something?" Peter fiddled with his mug.

"Sure."

"Your dad tells me you're here for a girl. Would I know her?"

Great. Dad had to go and spill the beans. Well, he was the one who connected him with the Franklins, so it was no surprise. Dad and Peter had met during their postgraduate studies way back in Sydney. So when Nick mentioned that Violet Reynolds lived in Trinity Lakes, Dad was on the phone faster than a croc chasing a runaway chook.

Violet Reynolds. The moment she walked into his life, he knew she was the one. His future wife. He had only spent a few hours with her, the best hours of his life, before she'd flown home to America. But Nick hadn't been able to put her out of his mind. They'd connected on a level that left him wanting to pursue it further. Much further.

When six months had passed and he still hadn't forgotten her for even a moment, he figured he should do something. She was the one. He knew it in his bones. It had to be a God thing, right? That's when the planning began. For the next six months he worked extra hours, saving every penny he could until he could make this trip.

Mum and Dad weren't happy when he told them.

"What about everything you've been working toward? You can't throw it all away on a whim."

"Dad, it's not like it's forever." Unless Violet felt the same way. "I'm only going there for a few months. Call it an extended vacation."

He didn't even bother addressing Dad's assumption that it was a whim. It wasn't. But Dad wouldn't understand.

Mum was more intuitive, yet she also had reservations. It was probably a shock to her, that her usually steady, easygoing son was going to up and leave for what seemed an ethereal ideal. "I don't want to see you get your heart broken, Nick." An expected argument from a mother. "She seems ... well ..."

"You think I'm punching above my weight?" Nick had winked at her. Of course, Mum had only seen photos of Violet on the internet, never met her in person like he had. Violet looked all glamorous, but the woman he'd met was as down-to-earth as they come. In a refined sort of way.

"That's not an issue, Trace." Dad sidled up behind her, wrapping his arms around her waist. "Everyone said you were out of my league. I still think they were right."

"Aw, hon, you've always been more than enough for me." Mum swiveled in his arms to give him a peck on the lips.

"Okay, you two." Nick laughed. "Do you need some privacy?"

Mum's face glowed with contentment as she turned back to face him, still in the circle of Dad's arms. He'd always loved watching their relationship and aspired to the same.

"Just make sure the Lord is guiding your steps, Nick. Not your heart or emotions." Mum's words pricked his conscience.

"That's what I'm doing, Mum." At least, he thought he was.

Reluctantly, after several discussions, some of them heated, his parents had agreed to let him go, with a promise that he'd check in with them regularly. And he'd obviously have to check in with Peter as well.

But it was a little embarrassing to admit. Nick had always scoffed at those who said the "God told me I'm going to marry that girl," kind of line. And now he had to come clean.

"Um ..." He picked up his pen and weaved it through his fingers. "Her name is Violet Reynolds."

Peter almost choked on his coffee, and his voice rose several decibels. "Pardon? Did you say Violet Reynolds?"

Nick looked in every direction in case anyone else heard. "Yeah. Why?"

"Do you realize who she is?"

"I know she lives in Trinity Lakes and works for a tourism

company." And that she's beautiful, like a real-life Princess Jasmine. Having three sisters ensured he'd seen plenty of Disney movies over the years.

"Yes, she works for The Reynolds Group." Peter raised his eyebrows.

Unease made Nick sit up straighter in his chair. "Should that mean something?"

Peter pressed his lips together in a thin line. "Her father is Morgan Reynolds."

"Morgan Reynolds?" Was he missing something? Well, he clearly was, by the way Peter emphasized the name.

"Only one of the biggest tycoons in the transport industry. Travelluxe Tours is one branch of that company, of which Violet Reynolds is the fresh new face." Peter shook his head. "You'll be lucky if you can get near her. I hate to say it, but I think you're wasting your time."

Nick's stomach dropped. A fool's errand. That's clearly what Peter thought. And the way he put it, it sounded daunting. He didn't know much about Violet Reynolds.

Peter must have seen the doubt in his face, because his expression softened. "Sorry I dumped that on you, son. Maybe it doesn't have to be a complete waste. There are plenty of single young people around here, many of them Aussies. I'm sure Lexi can introduce you."

"Yeah. It'll be cool." Although he wasn't looking for an Aussie. Not at all.

That night, when Nick was settled in his room, he pulled out his phone and checked the socials. There she was. Violet Reynolds. So vibrant. So full of adventure. So graceful. And despite Peter's words, Nick's firm sense of purpose remained. All he had to do was find her.

He quickly typed a lighthearted comment on one of Violet's posts. He never knew if she read his comments among the several hundred others, or if she even remembered who he was. Hopefully he'd meet her face-to-face again. Soon.

The next morning, after Mrs. Franklin insisted on packing him some snacks, he jumped in the compact car he had purchased and headed north to his part-time summer job, his first major drive on American roads. He planned to sell the car again just before he left. If he left. *Remember to stay on the right, sunshine.* It was about thirty minutes to the private runway that housed Freefall Adventures. Nick used to think flying in an airplane was the best until he jumped out of one. That feeling? There was nothing like it.

He pulled into the parking lot and entered the hangar.

"Nick Gordon, I presume? We didn't scare you off with all the waivers and requirements?" The man, probably in his late thirties, came forward to shake his hand.

Nick clasped his hand. "Not a chance. Mr. ... Martinez, wasn't it?"

"Yeah. But call me Frank. I take it you have your USPA membership and all the documents signed?"

Nick handed him a manila folder full of forms, including proof of his temporary United States Parachute Association membership.

"Great. Thanks."

Frank walked him over to a makeshift counter—nothing fancy about this office—deposited the folder, collected a clipboard, and gave Nick a brief tour of the facilities. There were a few tables where people could wait and eat snacks they purchased from vending machines in the corner. Board games littered the tables, and there were even a couple of old arcade games to amuse visitors. Bathrooms off to the side. And the equipment, all neatly hanging on one wall.

"First thing to do is familiarize yourself with the schedule. Here are the bookings for today." Frank handed Nick the clipboard.

Nick flicked through the pages. Three tandems plus some training. A full day. Excellent.

Wait. No, it couldn't be. Something caught his eye, and he flicked back to the first page. Violet Reynolds? What were the chances of that? Was there more than one person with that name in the area?

Nick raised his head at the sound of approaching voices and almost dropped the clipboard, his composure, and his dignity all at once. Violet Reynolds. In the flesh. Life was getting real. He wasn't prepared. He thought he'd have to search for her.

In what seemed like slow motion, she and her entourage headed for the counter and Frank, who then gestured towards Nick. Nick swallowed and his hands became slick, so he clutched the clipboard to his chest.

She was coming over. Violet Reynolds was coming over. To him.

Her face tipped up as she met his gaze, and a slight crease appeared between her pretty brows.

"Have we met?"

Nick's ability to speak puddled around his feet. "M ... maybe." Maybe? Definitely. He tried to rally. "Um. In Australia. Last year."

Violet's eyes widened, and a gasp left her. "You?"

Before he could say anything further, she swiveled back to Frank. "I'm going to need a new instructor."

CHAPTER TWO

Violet glanced back at the extremely tall, annoyingly good-looking Australian whose tanned face seemed a little ashen. And so it should. What he'd done twelve months ago was inexcusable. Hopefully, that expression he wore meant guilt. Lots of guilt.

But that wasn't how she was supposed to think anymore, was it? Jesus had saved her by grace, and apparently grace was what she should now be offering. It didn't come easy, though. She was still so new to Christianity. *Sorry, Lord.* She was not very good at it. Not at all.

Especially when one of the people who had caused her strife now stood right in front of her. It didn't matter how good-looking he was. He'd deceived her. Is that why she had been so gullible, so quick to make the wrong decision? He'd turned her head with that cute smile. Violet shoved the memories aside. How was he even here, anyway? There was no way she would allow him anywhere near her. Violet sent a speaking glance to Amelia. She would understand.

"I'm sorry, Ms. Reynolds. I don't have anyone else available," Frank answered her.

That was not an answer she could accommodate. "Can't I switch with Breanna's instructor?"

Frank looked embarrassed. "You could. But, unfortunately, her instructor hasn't arrived."

Violet wanted to give the man a serve about his team's lack of professionalism, but she held her tongue. "Are you saying only one of us will be jumping today?"

"I'm … er … well …" Frank cleared his throat then spoke in a more confident tone. "If you are concerned about Mr. Gordon's qualifications, I can assure you he is a very experienced skydiver and comes highly recommended."

"That may be so, but —"

"Nicky-Ned Flanders!" A booming voice cut across her. *Rude.* She swiveled to see another man enter the hangar. He aimed straight for the Australian with a laugh and a chest bump, which almost knocked Mr. Gordon off his feet. That would be a long way to fall.

"Mud? What are you doing here?" Mr. Gordon recovered his balance but seemed more shocked than before.

"Thought I'd join you for a while in the good old US of A."

This Mud also carried an Australian accent. Lovely. Two Australians. Just what she needed. Was Mud as dubious as Nick Gordon?

Mr. Gordon closed his eyes for a moment. Was he not pleased? What kind of name was Mud, anyway? Or Nicky-Ned Flanders, for that matter? Violet exchanged an amused glance with her friends.

Frank interjected with a cough. "Excuse me, Mr. Murchison. You're late."

"Yeah, sorry 'bout that. But just call me Mud." Mud lifted a fist as though he was expecting a fist bump, which he didn't receive.

"Right." Frank didn't appear impressed. "I'll need to see you after. Right now, paperwork, and let's get this show on the road."

While Mud rifled through his backpack and pulled out some crumpled documents, which he handed to Frank, Violet took the moment to step aside with Amelia.

"Did you know anything about this?" she whispered in her assistant's ear.

"About what?"

Violet gestured with her chin towards the tall hunk. "Mr. Australia. What's he doing here?"

Amelia turned wide eyes to her and matched her whisper. "I have no idea. I swear, I didn't know he'd be here. What are the odds?"

"So it's just a crazy coincidence?"

"Well ..." the word was long and drawn out. "There's something you should —"

"Ms. Reynolds," Frank called, ending their discussion. "Mike Murchison will be your instructor this morning."

The Mud character turned toward Violet and looked her up and down with an appraising wink. A shudder coursed through her. That kind of familiarity was discomfiting, to say the least.

"On second thoughts, now you've reassured me of Mr. Gordon's qualifications, I am willing to stay with him." Willing might be an overstatement. So much for not letting him anywhere near her. Better the devil you know, they say. Poor Bree. She would have to deal with the Mud fellow. Violet bit her bottom lip, trying not to smirk. Bree deserved it for suggesting this entire scheme.

Violet lifted her chin and headed over to Mr. Gordon. Better get this over with. She had to tilt her head back to meet his eyes. "So, Australia, it seems you are the one to teach me how to jump out of a plane."

He released what seemed to be a self-conscious chuckle. "Yeah."

"Nothing else? No extra services?" She couldn't hold back the sarcasm. God forgive her.

This man had given her, and Amelia and Tony—travel companions as supplied by her father—a wonderful tour of the Northern Territory. A scenic flight, lunch, and a road trip into Kakadu. All part of the service, he'd said. And on that basis, she had recommended the tour company to her father as one worthy of partnership. But it wasn't part of the service. He'd added on the lunch and drive to win the approval. And two months later Daddy was reaming her for recommending a sub-par organization.

A crease appeared on his brow and his Adam's apple bobbed. "Have I missed something? I am aware you're here to train to solo dive, if that's what you mean. After your first tandem dive today, you'll spend the rest of the weekend on the ground learning, followed by an exam. Wasn't that made clear to you?"

Violet sucked in her breath. So he was going to play innocent? "I am very clear on what is involved, thank you." He might pretend to be innocent, but she wasn't falling for his apparent genuineness twice.

She looked over her shoulder. Her friends were sitting at the tables, sipping sodas. Amelia was with them, furiously tapping away on her tablet with one hand, and making a phone call with the other. Bree was already being shown the equipment by Mud.

"Let's get started then, shall we?"

"Sounds like a plan. We have about an hour of training before we go up." Mr. Gordon moved over toward where parachutes lined the wall but seemed to fumble with everything he touched. Were his hands shaking? He even stuttered a little as he explained what everything was for.

Enough to make her doubt Frank's confidence in him.

"You have done this before, haven't you?"

"Huh? Yeah." Though his words were affirmative, he didn't

sound sure. "I, um, have over one thousand jumps under my belt."

Violet couldn't make sense of him. "Forgive my bluntness, but you seemed a lot more sure of yourself when you drove us down those off-road tracks in Kakadu." Would he take the hint, admit his duplicity?

"Huh, yeah." He ran a hand through his hair, self-conscious. Ashamed? "I didn't expect to see you here, that's all."

"I bet you didn't."

———

WHAT WAS HAPPENING? Not only had Nick been unprepared for Violet being here, he was completely unprepared for the accusation in her eyes, the indignation in her stance. Where had he gone wrong? Had he misread her enjoyment of the tour last year? Had he somehow offended her when he thought he was showing her and her team a good time?

And above all, had he been wrong in that conviction that she was the one? He closed his eyes momentarily. What a massive blunder that would be. He could imagine the "I told you so" stares from his parents, the pitiful shakes of the head of his other mates.

And what possessed Mud to follow Nick to the States? He'd be more trouble than it was worth, as much as he loved the guy. Nick hadn't even told him about Violet. How long would it take before Mud figured it out?

Nick opened his eyes to see Princess Jasmine in her hot-pink jump suit familiarizing herself with the rig and harness. That conviction was still there. Somehow, he had to figure out what she held against him. Later. Right now, he needed to focus on the safety of the jump. And show her he was confident and competent.

Pushing his shock aside, he drew a deep breath and led her

to a console to watch an instructional video. That would give him a breather to compose himself before he continued to teach her how to do the tandem jump.

While she watched, he strolled over to where Frank spoke through a handheld radio to the pilot, preparing for the first run. When he'd finished, Frank jerked his chin up. "What's up?"

Nick fidgeted with the zip on his suit. "Ms. Reynolds—did I read correctly—she's here for full training?"

Frank slapped him on the shoulder. "Yeah. She's in for the complete course. You'll be seeing a lot of her around here for the next few months. She's booked in several days per week for the summer."

Wow. A lifetime of Christmases on a silver platter couldn't have been better. Nick couldn't believe his luck. Or was it more than that? Was it a sign from the Lord? Whatever it was, he needed to make the most of it. Breathing out slowly, he returned to where Ms. Reynolds was just finishing the video.

"Time to get the harness on." He waved her over to the equipment rack.

Part of the job was to secure the harness she wore, which would then attach to him. He tried to push his attraction aside as he adjusted and tightened the straps at her thighs, her waist, and her shoulders. Too close. She smelled of vanilla and strawberries. And they would be even closer during the dive. But since she was averse to him at present, that wouldn't be a problem—well, not for her.

"When we're in freefall, it's very loud, so I'll communicate with you through hand signals." Nick forced his voice to steady.

"Okay."

"When we first leave the plane, you will have your hands here." He showed her how she should hold the shoulder straps.

"When we are clear of the plane, I will tap you on the shoulder. Then you can spread your arms wide." He did the movement and motioned for her to copy. Man, she was cute when she concentrated, her lips in a slight pout and a fine crease between her eyes.

He explained and showed her what would happen when they released the canopy and how she needed to position herself for the landing. The training sped by. Before he knew it, they were ready to board the Cessna and go up.

"Can I take my phone to grab some content on the way?" Violet blinked long dark lashes at him, which made his insides leap. She was going to be a hard one to deny anything. And while he understood social media was a big part of her work, for this job and safety …

"That's a hard no."

Violet's face fell. "Really?"

"Sorry, Ms. Reynolds, but it's too dangerous." Bah. Calling her Ms. Reynolds felt so formal. He wanted to be on friendly terms and call her Violet. Hopefully, the time would come for that. "The regulations don't allow a beginner to carry a phone or camera on a dive. You need to be licensed before you can do that. I'm surprised the staff didn't inform you during the booking process."

Violet chewed on her bottom lip. "Oh, my PA did all that for me." Nick could see the cogs turning in her lovely head. "But you're licensed, yes?"

"Correct." He grinned. "And I will have a camera attached to my arm throughout, so you can access that footage later."

Her shoulders relaxed. "Thank you."

Nick shrugged. "It's all part of the service."

Suddenly, Violet's eyes narrowed at him again. "Is it though?"

"Yes." Her suspicion knocked him off balance. Where did that come from? "But there is an extra charge."

Violet held his gaze for a moment, as if trying to ascertain if he was being truthful. Nick could get lost in those eyes if they weren't so full of antagonism. He broke the gaze and looked over her shoulder. Mud and Violet's friend were already boarding the plane. "Let's go." He motioned her toward the Cessna.

Inside the plane, he directed her to sit between his legs, her back against his chest so he could connect the harness. She hesitated for a moment, glancing over at the other two, already seated in a likewise manner. Why didn't she trust him? Not the best beginning for a skydive, that's for sure. Or for anything else.

She must have decided it was okay, as she turned and shuffled backward. Her fragrance filled his senses again, and the realization struck him with force. He was going to jump out of a plane with Violet Reynolds. His—hopefully—future wife. What a great story this would be in years to come. If he could convince her that he wasn't against her.

With everyone buckled in, the plane sped down the runway and lifted into the air. He'd never get over that feeling of the plane rising. Anticipation kicked in every time. Nick pulled his helmet on and checked over his equipment and harness connections again.

It was only a few minutes before they were close to the drop zone. He leaned forward to speak in Violet's ear.

"We have about sixty seconds of free-fall. Do you want to just fall straight, or would you like me to show you some maneuvers?"

Violet turned her head slightly toward him. So close. His heart leaped.

"What kind of maneuvers?"

"Somersaults, spins, that kind of thing."

"Why?"

Suspicion again. What was with her? "You strike me as the adventurous type." At least, she had been back in Australia. "I thought you might like something different. And you're aiming to dive solo. You might like to see what can be done."

"Sure." She turned her head away again. "Let's do that."

Nick frowned. "Is something wrong?"

"No. I'm fine." Her words were clipped.

"Are you having second thoughts?"

Some people got in the air and freaked out just before it was time, which was a waste. Thankfully, that wasn't a common occurrence.

"No."

He couldn't delve too deeply into what might be her problem. If there was a risk of conflict, it wouldn't be good for his concentration on the way down. He needed to be one hundred percent focused on the dive.

The pilot announced they were at the drop zone and Mud edged toward the open door with his partner. He shot a grin at Nick and gave him a thumbs up. "Blue skies."

Nick returned the gesture. It was a common saying amongst divers. And then they disappeared below the plane.

"You ready? It's our turn."

"Yes. All set."

Adrenaline surged. He pulled Violet toward the doorway, did a last check of the straps, and gave her a tap on the shoulder. "Three, two, one …"

CHAPTER THREE

The sudden rush of air against them was hard to describe. A loud roar filled her ears, as Nick Gordon had warned. But the sensation of flying was amazing. Not falling. Flying. Nick tapped her on the shoulder, and she released her arms wide as he'd shown her.

All of her wariness of his motivations left her in the free fall. She was in the moment. As promised, he rolled her and spun her several times. Exhilarating. She screamed, but it was a scream of delight. The earth below reeled in her vision as Nick somersaulted again. But before she knew it, he made signs to tell her he would pull the canopy, and their fall slowed to a gentle sail through the sky.

So beautiful. She looked down at the scenery below. Mountains covered with pine trees, the green fields of farms and ranches, and oh. "There's Trinity Lakes."

"Looks amazing from up here, doesn't it?"

The three pretty lakes glimmered in the summer sunshine, nestled at the foot of the mountains. The town seemed much smaller from up here. "It's glorious."

"I don't know the area well yet. Maybe you can point out some landmarks for me."

Her brain stalled. Why was Nick such a friendly guy? The same as he was in Australia. He seemed genuine then, and he seemed genuine now. But he wasn't. Well, that's what she'd believed afterward. Had she been wrong?

"It would help me give better service to other customers," Nick said when she didn't speak.

Violet sighed. She was enjoying this experience too much to sour it with meanness. She pointed. "That's the ski resort—see, on the mountain. And over there, by Lake Other—that's the summer camp."

"And that river over in the distance?"

"That would be Snake River, I assume."

Snakes. That triggered a powerful memory.

This man had handled a snake while they were in Kakadu. A massive—what did he call it?—Olive Python. He'd pulled over his four-wheel drive when he saw it on the road, casually strolled over and picked it up, like it was a pet kitten or something. He'd brought it over to the window and held it up to her.

"Wanna say hi? He won't hurt ya," he'd said. "He's a beauty, eh?"

Violet had wanted to recoil, but Nick was so calm, she'd impulsively trusted him and reached out a hand to touch the slithery creature. The scales were smooth under her fingers, but she sensed the power in its long, thick body.

"They like the warmth of the road to lie on," Nick explained as he took the python around to the others. Amelia shook her head, refusing to touch it, but Tony joined in without hesitation. Nick gave the snake a kiss and then released it beside the road, but not before she got some pics.

Violet would have to go back and have a look at those photos when she had a chance. Not that she wanted to relive any of that. He'd tricked her.

"Do you know which direction Seattle is from here?" Nick broke into her thoughts.

"Um …" She looked around, trying to get her bearings, and then pointed. "That way I think. Northwest."

"Great. Thanks."

"And if you look south, we're close to the Oregon border, and to Idaho in the east."

"Okay."

"Way over there on the horizon, probably more like northeast would be Spokane, but further north is the Canadian border."

"Fantastic." A breath. A soft chuckle. "I still don't know where I am."

Violet suspected he was talking about more than geography, but laughed nonetheless. "North America. Washington State. Trinity Lakes."

"Yeah, thanks. I thought it looked different from Australia, Northern Territory, Jabiru."

"What brought you over to the States?"

Silence for a long ten seconds. "Working holiday."

But why? Was he in trouble for what he did in Australia? Had he run away from the consequences? Is that why he looked panicked when she arrived this morning—she'd uncovered his hiding place? Maybe she should alert Daddy to his presence.

The ground accelerated toward them. Cars, then people, came into view. There were her friends on the ground, waving. Violet waved back. From the corner of her eye, she noticed Bree landing with Mud.

"Right. Legs up" Nick held his arms out to the side, ready to land.

Violet lifted her legs so he could do the landing work. A few seconds later, she stood on the ground as he released the harness. She couldn't help but admire his skill and turned to face him, even as her friends ran toward them. "That was amazing. Thank you." She could at least appreciate this experience, even if their previous encounter was clouded with deceit.

"You are very welcome." He pulled off his helmet, smiled into her eyes. "I'm stoked we met again today."

"Stoked?"

His light green eyes sparked. "That's Australian for happy."

So not panicked. Violet drew her brows together and opened her mouth to challenge him when Bree bounded at her, almost knocking her off balance.

"How amazing was that?"

"Incredible." Violet returned her embrace.

"I'm so pumped."

Lilly and Amelia caught up with them then, and Bree started gushing about her free fall experience while Violet nodded and grinned. Off to their right, Nick and Mud pulled in the parachutes and laughed together.

The group drifted back toward the hangar. Lilly and Amelia peppered them with questions, giving them barely room to take a breath.

"Are you still mad at me for making you go up with me, Bree?" Violet winked at her friend.

"I was never mad." Bree scowled. "Just a bit scared. But not anymore. I would do that again in a heartbeat."

"Well, I'll be glad for your company anytime you want to come out here with me." Violet squeezed her arm. "But I wouldn't expect you to do the whole training. It's pretty extensive."

"No, no. I'm happy to stick with the tandem dives." Bree's eyes swerved to Mud. No prizes guessing where her motives lay.

Violet turned to Amelia. "Speaking of extensive, perhaps we'll only ask our contacts to do a group tandem dive. There's no sense in asking them to do as much work as me. I'll try to organize the formation dive with a few pros. I didn't realize what a huge commitment this would be. While I can manage it, they may not be able to."

"No problem, Vi." Amelia tap-tapped on her tablet. "I was thinking of a couple of locals who could help. Adam Lancaster has a big following on his podcast. Mitchell Reilly, the hockey player. Heidi Klassen would be good, though not as fun to deal with. I asked Liam Darcy, but he declined. He did offer to throw a generous donation our way. I'll also throw the net wider to some celebrities you've had contact with."

The girls squealed and clapped at the idea.

"What cause are you going to promote?" Lilly asked.

Violet sobered. "I've heard a lot about trafficking lately. I've found an organization called Haven of Hope who rescue trafficked girls and help them build a new life. I haven't contacted them yet, but I think they would be a good organization to support."

"Yeah, that sounds great," Lilly nodded.

"Free fall for freedom," Breanna clapped.

"Yes," Violet almost shouted. "What a perfect name. Let's do this."

"I'll get onto it straightaway." Amelia grinned.

The girls all hugged her. Soon, Amelia, Bree and Lilly headed back to Trinity Lakes, while Violet stayed to continue her training.

She looked around to see where Nick and Mud had got to but couldn't see them. They were obviously off training new clients for the next tandem. She knew a twinge of disappointment but couldn't fathom why. Nick had some explaining to do.

But she hardly saw him for the rest of the day. He went from one customer to the next, and she was often busy taking in the instructions of another trainer. She forced herself to focus. Missing important details in this training could mean life and death. She would have to catch up with Nick Gordon another time.

———

"Where are you staying?" Nick asked Mud as they headed toward the parking lot.

"The campground."

"You mean the RV park?" Nick grinned, correcting Mud's Australian terminology. "I'll follow you, then." Nick pressed the remote and folded himself into the tiny hatchback.

"What the …?" Mud released an expletive. "Is that your car?"

"It's not like I'm planning to tour the country. It was afford-able." Two excuses Mud would probably not appreciate.

"Yeah, about that …"

"We'll talk back in your cabin." Nick didn't want to get into it right there, but he definitely wanted to know why Mud had shown up today.

"Fine. Well, enjoy your matchbox." He laughed as he unlocked a beefy black pickup. "Cabin number three," he called over his shoulder as he fishtailed out of the driveway in a spray of gravel. Frank probably wouldn't appreciate that behavior. But what would you expect from an industry of adrenaline junkies?

Nick swiveled his head for one last look toward the hangar. Had Violet finished yet? He wanted to talk to her properly, to find out what was eating her. He sighed. No sign of her. So he'd deal with Mud first.

On his way into town, he stopped to grab a couple of pizzas. Mud wouldn't have any food. Mud rarely thought ahead. Nick sent a quick text to the Franklins to let them know he might be late getting back and headed around to the RV park and camping ground. A pretty spot sprawled along the lakefront, the late afternoon sun reflecting warm colors from its glassy surface. He remembered Violet pointing out this park to him from the air that morning. It had been awesome being that close to her, yet frustrating, not knowing why she was so wary around him.

Nick knocked on cabin three's door.

"Come in," Mud yelled from somewhere within. He stepped inside the small two-roomed building and put the pizza on the coffee table, then sank into a two-seater sofa. "I brought dinner."

"Awesome." Mud appeared from the bathroom, one towel tied around his waist, rubbing his hair dry with another. "Just give me a sec."

He disappeared into the bedroom and emerged moments later, dressed in ripped jeans and a t-shirt, his hair still damp, a mess of uncombed waves.

Nick opened a pizza box and grabbed a slice. "Spill, Mud. How is it you turn up here a week after me, and rock into the same skydive business?" He took a bite and watched his friend.

Mud selected a slice of pizza and took an oversized bite. "We'll probs need to make this quick," he said around a mouthful of pizza. "My body's telling me it's the middle of the night, and my head's spinning."

"So talk."

"Well, I was kinda in between jobs."

Nothing new there. Mud struggled to settle into one place for a long time. He was a mechanic by trade and did other jobs on the side.

"Anyway, I went around to your place to catch up. How come you never told me you were coming to the States?"

Nick narrowed his eyes. "Probably for the exact reason you're sitting here."

"Your folks told me you're here for a girl."

There it was.

"At first I didn't believe them," Mud continued. "That's just crazy talk. You'd never do something so spontaneous."

"Believe me, it wasn't spontaneous." Months of vacillating, then months of planning. No, not impulsive at all.

"Well, I figured I'd better come and keep an eye on ya. Make sure you don't do something stupid."

Great. Just great. This was going to be extra fun. Nick sighed and took another bite of his pizza. But Mud was a good friend, his best friend in truth, and probably had his best interests at heart, even though it would probably be Mud who needed to be watched.

"Anyway, I'm only here for a month. Gotta go back to help with the burn offs."

Another of Mud's side jobs. Firefighting. And in the dry season, they did a lot of controlled burns in the Top End.

"So who's the girl?"

Nick washed his pizza down with some cola. "You met her today." This would be interesting. "She was my first tandem jump."

"The hot chick in the hot pink?"

Nick nodded and grinned.

"But she doesn't even like you."

"Thanks for the encouragement." Nick frowned. He didn't need to be reminded. Anyway, there must be some misunderstanding. He'd get it sorted.

"So what are we doing tomorrow?" Mud asked.

"I dunno about you, but I'm going to church."

"Yeah, nah. You can have that one for yourself." Mud had never shown an interest in Nick's faith, though Nick continually prayed for his friend.

Half an hour later, he said goodbye to Mud, seeing as the guy was drifting to sleep whilst they talked.

"Sorry, dude. Can't stay awake," Mud had said as he rose from the sofa and backed toward the single room.

Outside the cabin, the lure of the still, quiet waters of the lake called him, and he strolled down to the shore. In the darkness, and checking no-one was around, he stripped down to his underwear and waded in. His breath sucked in at the coolness of the water. Well, freezing really, compared to the warm tropical waters of the Northern Territory. Minutes later, refreshed but cold, he pulled his clothes over his wet body and headed to his car.

Back at the Franklins, the house was quiet. They'd probably all gone to bed, ready for an early start at church the next morning. Nick should do the same.

He sent a quick message to his parents since it was still too early in the morning in Australia for them to be up yet. Then he opened the socials to see what Violet had posted for the day. Yes, there was an image captured from his wrist-cam of the two of them midair, a huge grin on her face and a big thumbs up. The caption read "Free fall for Freedom" and there was a link to a donation page with further information on an organization which fought human trafficking. Her resolve to turn something fun into a way to help people moved him. Yes, he could easily fall for this woman. In fact, he was already halfway there.

Nick flicked back to her social page and added a comment to the photo, which already had thousands of likes and several hundred comments. *Loved jumping with you today. Looking forward to the next one.*

He lay awake for a while, trying to figure out what might have set Violet against him, but came up with nothing. The one day they'd spent together had been perfect in every way. He needed to get her on her own and talk to her, hopefully between jumps the next time their schedules crossed paths.

Except, the next morning, when he slipped into the Trinity Lakes Community Church slightly late, he was sure Princess Jasmine stood near the front as the worship band played. Even though he could only see her from behind, he was certain it was her. He didn't even know she was a Christian. Bonus. *Thank you, Lord.* And she was at the same church? It couldn't be chance, could it?

Nick edged into one of the back rows and tried to focus on

the worship, although his palms seemed to be suddenly coated with sweat. A few people looked his way and nodded a greeting, but he didn't know anybody yet. He wiped his hands down his jeans and smiled back. Despite his nerves, despite being on the other side of the world, attending church still felt like coming home. There was something about being in the global church family that produced an instant connection, and the worship drew him in, many of the songs familiar.

After the worship, a pastor got up and promoted a few upcoming events, encouraging people to connect in home groups, all the familiar routine Nick remembered from home. He smiled, contented, and looked forward to the message.

"Before we come to the word this morning," the pastor said, "we have a special testimony from one of our new sisters in Christ. Please welcome Violet Reynolds."

What? Oh wow. This was going to be awesome.

Violet stood and climbed the few steps to the platform, her perfectly form-fitting navy dress flowing gracefully around her ankles. She took the microphone from the pastor and placed a tablet on the lectern, then looked up and smiled. Oh, that smile …

"Good morning, everyone. Most of you probably know me by now, but you wouldn't be aware of the journey I've been on over the past year." She cleared her throat, a gentle sound. "Even from my childhood, I have struggled with my identity as a person. Early last year, something took place in my personal life that caused me to organize a trip to Australia. I used a business trip as cover, but in reality, I was in pursuit of that which I thought was lacking in my life.

"When I arrived in Australia, I quickly discovered I was chasing a fantasy. With that failure clawing at me, I continued my trip and business in the north of Australia. Again, what I thought to be reality, I soon learned, was empty and false. All of it made me question who I was all over again."

Nick frowned. What had happened to her? He wanted to know, more than ever.

"Back home, the consequences of that trip piled up. I lost confidence and focus. I lost purpose and wondered what I was here for." She drew a deep breath. Those words were clearly hard to say, though they came out calm and clear.

"A good friend of mine took me to the healing services over at Trinity Life Church at Easter. That's when I learned about Jesus and his sacrifice on the cross. I gave my heart to the Lord pretty quickly after that. I'm still learning, but I am so glad I am on this new path, and so glad to have a new family who encourages me in every step."

She paused and gazed across the room, her eyes scanning past him, stopping, swerving back to him, and her lips parted in a faint gasp. She stared at him momentarily before she recovered and cleared her throat again.

"Thank you." She handed the microphone back to the pastor and left the stage.

Had she been going to say more? Did she cut her talk short because she saw him? More than ever, he wanted to get close to her and clear the air.

CHAPTER FOUR

W hat was Nick Gordon doing here? Was he following her? How would he even know she was here? The only people who knew her plans for today were Tony and Alistair, and neither of them would have mentioned it to anyone. Would they? Thank goodness she had almost finished her testimony before she noticed him. And thank goodness she hadn't shared the details of what he'd done in Australia, hadn't named him or anything. As much as she was annoyed at him, she wasn't into public shaming.

Violet resisted the urge to look over her shoulder while Pastor Dean spoke. Why she even wanted to look at the man was beyond her. She was angry now. Did he claim to be a Christian? Yet went around duping innocent people? That was worse than if he didn't know the Lord at all.

Violet shook her head. He wasn't worth wasting energy on. She forced herself to listen to Pastor Dean's message, which challenged her. He was talking about how as the world gets darker, believers need to shine their light brighter, to show Jesus to others through both their words and lifestyle. Her stomach knotted. As yet, she hadn't told her friends about her new faith, not even Amelia. Amelia just knew Violet was going to church. She chewed on her lip, knowing this was something she should remedy.

As soon as the service was over, Violet made a beeline for the door. Alistair would be in the parking lot, waiting to take her out for lunch. She only hoped she could get out before Mr. Australia tried to speak to her. She didn't want to deal with him today.

Relief flooded her as Pastor Dean approached him before she headed down the aisle. She didn't even want to look at him but couldn't help herself. Why did he have to be so darned good looking? He wore his hair down today, the first time she'd seen it like that, as he usually wore it tied up in a topknot. Well, the two times that she'd met him. But long brown coils fell past his shoulders. From a distance, it almost appeared like dreadlocks. He sported an ivory blazer and washed jeans, and he was looking her way, raising his eyebrows and chin in a friendly greeting. Ugh.

Violet tore her gaze away to almost collide with another member of the congregation. "Oh, sorry." She jerked to a stop.

"It's okay." the young woman giggled. "I just wanted to say thank you for sharing this morning."

Violet knew her from the cell group she attended. "Thank you, Clare."

"You've got me thinking," Clare said, nodding. "Are you coming this Wednesday? Do you think you could share a little more about your journey?"

"I'd love to." Violet reached out and put a hand on Clare's forearm and smiled. "Can we chat a bit later? I have someone waiting for me outside." Indeed, her phone was vibrating in her purse. Probably Alistair asking where she was. "Thanks for the encouragement."

Alistair took her to the country club for lunch. No surprises there. It was pretty much the only place he would take her in

Trinity Lakes. He looked down his nose at this town she loved, like it was beneath him. He'd flown in to see her for the day and would fly out again that evening. Alistair lived in Seattle like her father, more comfortable with city life than a cute tourist town amongst scenery.

Sure, he was good-looking, but she watched him scrolling his phone while they ate. They were both there at the will of their fathers, it seemed. Two magnates who wanted to merge in more ways than one. Violet sighed as she forked smoked salmon into her mouth. It was a far cry from the laughing lunch she had shared with Nick Gordon last year. Nick had her, Amelia, and Tony in stitches, to the point she almost sprayed coffee all over the table. The fact the coffee came out of her nose sent the others into further peals of laughter. So undignified. So against her father's expectations and training.

And why was she even thinking about Nick Gordon? He was the bane of her existence. She was angry at him. So angry. Even if part of her believed sitting across from him at lunch would be preferable to Alistair's company.

"How's your week been?" Violet pushed thoughts of the Australian aside.

"You should see the projection figures we generated." His eyes lit up, and a broad grin stretched his mouth. Violet couldn't help but respond with her own smile. He was rather cute when animated like this.

Alistair launched into a description of all the graphs and charts he created while making economic projections. At least he was excited about it, but Violet's interest waned quickly.

What would he think if she told him about the skydiving? No, he would probably run and tell Daddy. She'd already posted it on social media, so they could find it if they wanted to. If they followed her. The fact he never mentioned it spoke reams.

Alistair was a good man. Just as Lyall had been. Lyall. The boy she grew up with. Her neighbor. Her best friend. The boy who, as an eight-year-old, had told her he would marry her one day. The boy whose parents seemed to expect the same. The boy she had dated for a few months—never mind that they were only fifteen.

She'd followed him to Australia, little knowing he was running away from his family's pressure on him. Thoughtlessly, she'd mentioned her close relationship with him to everyone she met in the small country town. Until she found out he'd met and proposed to someone else. She'd almost ruined Lyall's new relationship with her naivety and impulsiveness. Devastated, ashamed and confused, she'd hightailed it to Darwin and onto that disastrous tour with Nick Gordon.

The red explosive look on Daddy's face appeared in her mind. When he learned what had transpired in Australia, he'd lost it. Why would she throw away her future, chasing after a man who had no future in their world of transport and travel? Lyall was a dentist, for crying out loud. Then allowing herself to be manipulated by a con man posing as a tour guide, to try and land a lucrative contract. No. No. No. She needed to open her eyes. To think before she acted. To do the opposite of what was in her head. And in that moment, her already thin confidence was shattered.

Surreptitiously, Violet checked her phone for the time. Several hours to go before Alistair left for his flight. She looked back up at him and pasted on a polite smile, trying to feel more interest in him and everything he talked about. Violet was clueless about how to choose the right partner. Australia made that clear. Daddy believed Alistair was the one, and she would do her best.

When Monday morning arrived, so did Amelia, right on nine o'clock, as she did every day. Even though Daddy had pretty much grounded Violet for the summer, giving her time to regain her balance while he decided what to do with her after her continuous blunders, there was still other work to do as part of her tourism role. Networking. Creating new contacts. Researching new tour companies and what they offered. Seeking to find luxurious tours that would fit with the Travel-luxe brand.

"Before we get to work," Amelia said. "There's something I need to talk to you about."

"Sure." Violet poured them both a coffee. "What is it?"

They sat at the breakfast bar with their steaming coffees and Amelia pulled out her tablet, woke it up and started tapping on apps.

"Nick Gordon," she said.

Violet's stomach did a little flip-flop, and she frowned. That man's name should not have that effect on her. "What about him?"

"Do you remember when that Mud fellow came into the hangar on Saturday?"

"Yes."

"And he called him Nicky-Ned?"

"Yes. An odd nickname, don't you think?"

"I agree. But as soon as I heard it, something triggered in my memory." She turned the tablet around so Violet could see it clearly. "*Nicky-Ned* aka Nick Gordon has been following you on the socials since we went to Australia. I didn't realize it was him all this time, as he uses a picture of Shrek as his avatar."

A twinge of fear shot through Violet. "What do you think it means? Is he stalking me? Is this one of those twisted fan nightmares you see in the movies?"

Amelia pressed her lips together and shook her head. "I'm not getting that vibe. He's been posting comments on our content almost daily, but nothing creepy at all."

"Show me."

Amelia tapped on a few different posts and scrolled to find comments.

Looks like you had a great day.

Nice scenery.

That must have been a fun adventure.

Like Amelia said, nothing weird.

"But when I look at his profile, there's not much there. Very few friends or anything." Amelia added.

"So it is weird?" Unease still vibrated through Violet.

"Maybe. Maybe not." Amelia chewed on her lip.

"There's more?"

"Well, yesterday afternoon, he actually sent a direct message."

Violet shivered involuntarily. "So should I be alarmed? Do I need to call the police? Or Tony?"

Amelia chewed her lip again. "I'm not a hundred percent sure, but it might be worth reading first."

Violet stared into her friend's eyes, trying to read if she was fearful as well. All she recognized was uncertainty. "All right. Let me see it then."

More tapping on the tablet, then Amelia handed it to her.

Hi Violet. I was pretty stoked to see you in church today, but when I heard your testimony, I knew we needed to talk. I get the strong impression that something I've done has caused you grief, and I am at a loss to know what I've done. I would really appreciate it if we could catch up sometime soon and hopefully clear this up. Please know I would never intentionally do anything to cause you harm (or anyone else, for that matter). Maybe you could come early to your next skydiving lesson? See you soon, Nick.

Violet lifted her gaze to meet Amelia's eyes. "He doesn't know? How can that be?" She hopped up from the bar stool and paced behind the counter. "He must be lying. Don't you think?"

Amelia shrugged.

"What? You have no advice?"

She shrugged again. "I don't know. All I can say is he seemed genuine then, and he seems genuine now. So —"

"So, either he's very good at misleading people, or ... or what?" Violet didn't want to acknowledge the other option.

"Maybe we've completely missed something?"

"I don't see how." But the only way to get closure on this was to have it out with him. If that's what he wanted, that's what he'd get. She went back to the breakfast bar, picked up the tablet, and typed a reply.

"Are you sure about this?" Amelia's eyes were wide.

Violet nodded. "I'll get Tony to drive me. He'll keep an eye on Nick Gordon."

———

Nick was unaccountably nervous as Mud drove him to the hangar on Wednesday morning. Well, it wasn't really unaccountable. Violet had agreed to meet with him, and now he was stressed about the outcome. Her message was curt, to say the least.

Wednesday. 8:30 a.m.

But it was something. Now to learn what ate at her. What had he done to upset her world so much that she went looking for answers in Christ? Yes, it was great she'd found Jesus. Yes, it was great to know he'd had a hand in her salvation. But he'd rather she'd found Jesus through him doing something right, not something wrong.

"Man, will you stop fidgeting?" Mud crunched the gear change.

"What? I'm just ..." Just what? Fiddling with a hairbrush Mud had left in his center console. He groaned and dropped it, putting his hand under his thigh to hold it still. The half hour drive felt much longer this morning.

"It'll be fine, dude. Chill."

"Mm-hm." Nick didn't feel like arguing or even conversing. He closed his eyes and thought back on telling Peter Franklin how Violet Reynolds had literally fallen into his lap, harnessed to him for a tandem jump. Then she'd been in church.

Peter suggested it was a coincidence. Nick wanted to believe the Lord was bringing Violet across his path.

Peter had sighed and asked the all-important question. "You won't do something stupid like tell her God told you to marry her, will you?"

Dad had said something similar when they caught up on the phone. Did they both think he was a complete weirdo? He got the message. Don't come on too strong.

It was hard to stop his hopes from soaring, now they had a chance to clear the air. Assuming he hadn't actually done something wrong back in Australia.

They finally pulled up in the parking lot, and Nick almost tripped over his legs climbing out of the truck. Two left feet today.

"Nick."

A greeting came from across the lot. Nick straightened and squinted against the morning sunshine to see Tony, Violet's chauffeur, security guy, or whatever he was, leaning on a car. So that was how it was going to be.

Nick turned to Mud. "See you in there." He slung his backpack over his shoulder and strode over to the dark gray Mercedes with tinted windows, then put out his hand to shake. "Tony."

Tony grasped his hand with a firm grip and slapped him on the shoulder. "Good to see you, man."

"You too." Nick glanced around to see where Violet might be.

"She's in here." Tony straightened and opened the rear door. "Get in."

"Right. Ta." Movies about the mafia flashed through his head as Nick dropped his backpack and slid into the back seat. Tony closed the door behind him.

His nerves kicked up a notch as vanilla and strawberry filled his senses. Sunglasses covered her eyes, so he couldn't read her expression. Couldn't tell if she was receptive to him. All he could do was play it cool.

"Morning." That was a beginning.

"Hi."

"So where do we start?" Nick wasn't sure what to say or ask.

"You can start by explaining why you tricked me into recommending a contract with Top End Sky View." Her tone was terse, uncompromising. She obviously believed it, but he had no idea what she was talking about.

"Hang on. What contract?"

Even with the sunglasses, he could see her brows draw together. "I was there to experience the scenic flight with the view to sign a partnership with TESView."

"Were you? I didn't know that." This was all news to Nick.

"How could you not know? It seems your boss gave you extra incentive to look after us."

Now it was Nick's turn to frown. "No. He's not even—"

"Come on, Mr. Gordon. Just be straight with me. What were all those extra services about? I know for a fact that lunch and a tour into Arnhem Land are not part of the service."

Wow. She had gone super formal on him. This was serious. What had happened?

Violet waited for an answer with her arms folded across her chest. "Well?"

He swallowed a ball of trepidation and fiddled with the zipper on his jumpsuit. "He's not my boss—the guy who runs TESView. I was filling in for the day. For Mud, actually. You can ask him. Mud had an interview and asked me to fill his morning shift as tour-guide."

Violet sat in silence, absorbing this news. She opened her mouth and closed it a few times. It would be easy enough for her to verify what he was saying, which she probably knew.

"So why the extra treatment? If you weren't put up to it by TESView, why go out of your way?"

Nick sucked in a deep breath and toyed with the zip. Truth time. He released a self-conscious chuckle with his breath. "Well, um, I … I thought you were pretty and cool and … I guess I wanted to hang out some more. Show you a good time." He chanced a glance up to her face but couldn't read anything with those darned sunnies on.

Violet's lips pressed into a thin line. "All three of us?"

What would it take to convince her? "I couldn't very well leave the other two stranded. Besides, I could tell Tony was unlikely to be parted from you. Tell me I'm wrong."

Violet sat quietly, not answering.

"Did TESView even know that's what you were there for? I mean, they're a small out-of-the-way tourism organization. I didn't know who you were, and I suspect they didn't either."

"Give me a minute." Violet opened the door and got out. When minutes ticked by and she hadn't returned, Nick began to toy with the door handle. Should he wait? In the end, he got out of the vehicle to find Violet standing by the car on the other side, her phone to her ear.

On seeing him, she ducked back inside the car. Nick turned to Tony. "Should I …?" He gestured to the car. Tony shrugged. Unsure, Nick opened the door again and got back in.

Without warning, the glasses were off, and Violet had her face in her hands. Was she … crying?

"Miss Reynolds?" The formality made him uncomfortable, but he didn't have enough credibility to be informal. "Are you okay?"

"I'm sorry. I've been blaming you this whole time, but it's me who's the problem. I'm just not good at my job, and I didn't want to admit it was my fault." Her voice cracked. "You are right. I was there to evaluate TESView, but they didn't know it at all."

Nick wanted to comfort her but wasn't sure how. Hesitantly, he put a hand on her shoulder. "Hey. It's not all on you. I should have been more up-front."

Violet lifted tear-filled eyes to him and her mouth twitched into a smile. "That's gracious of you. But if you'd told me you just wanted to hang out, I would have said no."

"Right." Disappointment surged in him.

"And I'd have missed out on a great time. I'm sorry. I've been angry with you for an entire year, for no reason."

Relief whooshed through Nick. It seemed she believed him. "Well, then. Does that mean … do you think we can be friends now?"'

"You've seen me cry. I think we have to be." She let out a wobbly laugh. "Give me five minutes to sort myself out. Then I'll meet you in the hangar."

As promised, she walked into the hangar a few minutes later, to all appearances like nothing had happened. He led her through the next phase of training to prepare for a consolidation dive. This time he and Mud would hold on to her all the way down and get her to work through some actions she'd learned.

It seemed like the day flew by until they were inside the plane, heading up to the drop zone. She sat next to him this time, not harnessed to him, while Mud was further toward the front of the plane, talking to the pilot.

Nick nudged Violet gently with his elbow. "So you think I'm a pretty good tour guide?" He wiggled his eyebrows at her and grinned. Such a goof.

She giggled, her gaze dropping demurely. "I suppose." Then she looked back up at him, and her face lit up with a wide smile.

The force of his attraction hit him hard, and all sense left him. Lost in her eyes, words came of their own accord.

"Will you marry me?" Wait. What? Did that just come out of his mouth? After assuring others he wouldn't be weird. Nick groaned. Precious. That was the closest he'd ever get to swearing. *Lord, save me.*

The smile disappeared from Violet's face faster than a lightning strike. "Pardon?"

Hopefully, the roar of the Cessna's engine would cover his stupidity. "Will … *would* … would you … *your* … marketing team … be open to some ideas for the big finale?

Violet stared at him for a moment as if piecing together the truth, and then she shrugged. "Sure. Why not?"

Great. Now he just had to come up with the ideas. The pilot announced they were in the drop zone. Thank goodness for timing. "We'll chat later."

Mud moved closer, and the three of them edged to the doorway.

Violet looked down and looked nervous.

"It's okay. You're quite safe." Nick took her hand.

"Mm-hm." She pressed her lips together.

"We could push you out and you'd have no choice but to trust us to guide you down. But I want you to take the leap. Trust. You can trust me, Violet."

CHAPTER FIVE

Violet entered her home that afternoon, pausing at the kitchen counter, phone in hand. She dropped her purse and keys on the countertop and opened her messaging app. She started typing a message to Nick.

Had fun today. Would you like to meet for coffee ...

And what? Talk about his ideas for the formation dive event? No. She deleted the text. There was too much to process. She didn't need to act on every whim that came into her head.

Think first. Act later. Think first. Act later.

Whatever is in your head, do the opposite.

She put her phone down and moved to the lounge, sinking onto the sofa. So Nick wasn't the bad guy after all. A simple phone call with Amelia and her speedy research had confirmed Nick hadn't been on TESView's payroll. He had been contracted for that one day, and that was it. She'd ignored her own faults, unwilling to be reprimanded by her father. Unwilling to see the disappointment in his eyes. Unwilling to prove him right ... again. Violet groaned. Why did she have to be so impulsive? Because a cute guy with a man bun and a goofy smile treated her to a pleasant day?

Who was she kidding? Pleasant didn't cut it. The day had been fantastic. The best.

In fact—Violet got up and hurried to her room—she had written about it in her travel journal, hadn't she? She rifled through her bedside drawer. Yes, there it was. She sat on the bed and scooted back against the pillows, flicking through the pages till she found the entry for Kakadu.

Goodness, she had written a lot.

Today is just what I needed after the fiasco with Lyall. Our tour guide, Nick Gordon, made us laugh so hard and so often, I forgot all my troubles. The scenery from the air over Kakadu was breathtaking. Majestic cliffs and waterfalls, flooded plains, a vast landscape beneath us. Nick explained everything, including the native Dreamtime stories, and answered our questions confidently. From the air, we could see our hotel, built to resemble a giant crocodile, nestled amongst the trees.

She'd gone on to write the details about their hilarious lunch, with Nick telling them story after story. Then he'd taken them in a four-wheel drive just inside Arnhem Land. He navigated a river crossing with ease, perhaps even relish, pointing out a crocodile lurking in the reeds near the bank.

Violet laughed as she read about the python incident. After releasing the snake, he'd come back to the car. "I've got another snake in my esky if you wanna see it."

Curious enough now, Violet had jumped out and headed around to the back of the Land Cruiser to see what Nick had in store. He opened the back and put his hand on the lid of an icebox.

"That's an esky?"

"Don't you call it that?"

Violet had shaken her head and giggled.

"Well, this snake is a taipan. A bit more of a deadly sort, so we've gotta be careful opening this up." His eyes sparked. This guy loved his reptiles. "You ready?"

"Okay." Violet took a step back, a little wary.

Nick lifted the lid of the cooler and a snake literally flew out. Violet had screamed and run away. But when she turned back, Nick stood there with a rubber snake dangling from the lid, chuckling like a child.

"Oh." She'd wanted to hit him, but had joined him laughing instead, as did Tony and Amelia.

"I wish I'd caught that on camera," Tony said.

"Is this a prank you play on every unsuspecting tourist?" Violet asked.

Nick looked amused and unrepentant. "Pretty much."

Violet read the rest of the entry with a grin stretching her mouth. Goodness, she'd even drawn a little love heart at the end.

What was she supposed to do with all this? She could have sworn he proposed to her on the plane. But maybe she misheard. Or was that what she wanted to hear? Because the thing that scared her was that it didn't scare her, not in the least. It was perhaps the most natural thing he might have said. What was that about? Was it even normal?

Violet groaned again. No. She was seeing Alistair. Daddy would know better how to choose a partner for her—he was outside all the tangled emotions. Outside all the emotions and instincts she couldn't trust. Had never been able to trust. Had been told made her less than. Silly. Unreliable.

So, when they'd landed their parachutes today, Violet had approached Nick. She had to stop this before it started. She owed him the truth.

"I should probably tell you I'm seeing someone."

For a second, she thought maybe she'd been wrong ... again. But when his face fell, she figured she was right after all.

But he recovered quickly.

"None of my business. I'm happy for you. Really." Yet he seemed uncomfortable and fumbled with his chute. "I'd better

… I'll get this stuff inside." He excused himself and took off with long strides.

Violet watched his retreating form with a little regret. He seemed like a great guy, and something about him drew her. But she couldn't trust herself. It would be just like her to ruin everything. Again.

Yet today, when Nick had whispered in her ear to trust him, it was as though those words blew right into her soul. She did trust Nick. She had from the minute she'd met him in Australia, even when it looked like she shouldn't. Hadn't she always been taught her instincts were wrong? Undependable?

Today, it was as though another voice, a higher voice, was encouraging her to trust. It was more than trusting Nick to help her land safely. It was about trusting that the Lord had her future in His hands.

Violet tossed aside her journal and picked up her Bible. Yes, she should probably focus on that more. Pastor Dean said the Bible was her foundation, something solid when everything around her felt like shifting sand. What was that verse he'd mentioned? Matthew chapter seven? She flicked through the pages until she found what she was looking for. Ah yes, the wise and foolish builders. Pastor Dean had said she needed to build her life on the Word of God, which would give her the strength to stand when difficulties come. *Thank you, Jesus. Help me lean on your Word.*

"YOU WANNA CATCH A MOVIE TONIGHT?" Mud asked Nick as they drove home. "I mean, now you know your girlfriend is, well, not your girlfriend."

"Thanks for rubbing it in, mate." That knowledge had been an enormous blow. There had been nothing about a boyfriend in any of Violet's socials. Not even a photo of her with a guy other than Tony or a man he assumed was her father. And to top it off, why should Mud derive so much pleasure from the news?

"See? That's what I mean. You need to hang out with me to nurse your bruised ego. We can go to the pub and down a few pints."

"Come on, man." Nick rolled his eyes. "You know I don't drink." But the bruised ego was right. Well, bruised hope was more like it. It was easy for Mud. He attracted girls like blowies to a barbecue, or flies to a grill, as the Americans would have it. He was already cozying up to Breanna, Violet's friend. Probably nothing serious, since he was leaving in a few weeks.

"Okay." Mud put on an American accent. "We can go to the diner and have fries and a soda."

Nick could not help but grin at Mud's antics. "Sure, let's do that. But I'm going to Bible study later. You can join me if you like."

"Yeah, nah." Mud parked in the main street near Joe's Diner. "I'm gonna hit the gym for a workout."

That sounded about right. Mud loved working on his physique. Inside the diner, they found a booth and ordered their food.

"What are you gonna do about your Disney princess?" Mud winked. Nick had told him about his Princess Jasmine comparison.

Nick leaned back in his seat and fiddled with the drink coaster. He let out a sigh. "Yeah, I dunno." He really didn't. He wouldn't disrespect her by pursuing something if she weren't available. "At least we're friends now, I guess."

A waitress brought their food over. Mud took a huge bite of his burger, then spoke before he'd finished chewing. "Come on, man. You just gotta turn up the charm." He wiggled his eyebrows.

Nick gave him a scathing look as he sucked on his straw, but he didn't comment. Mud wouldn't care much about treading on someone else's toes. He would just move in and take his chances. Nick didn't operate like that. Didn't want to operate like that. But Mud wouldn't understand putting the outcome in God's hands, so there wasn't much to say.

"So what? Are you just gonna pack up and go home?" Mud asked between mouthfuls.

"No." Definitely not. "I'll see out the summer here, just as planned." And he'd see what happened. If this was truly a God thing, then He would make it happen.

———

NICK ENTERED the address Clare had given him on Sunday into the GPS and headed to her place. It would be good to be around other like-minded people. He loved Mud to death, but Mud never understood matters of faith, and didn't always get matters of integrity. Nick wished Mud would accept Jesus, but he continued to resist, saying he didn't need a savior—he was all good.

"I'm so glad you came." Clare beamed as she opened the door. "Come in. This way."

"Thanks for inviting me." Nick ducked past her and followed her directions.

He stopped dead at the entry to the room. Dining chairs, a sofa and two armchairs encircled a coffee table laden with snacks and drinks, and only one seat remained empty. Right next to Violet Reynolds. How was it they kept turning up in the same places? *Is this you, Lord?*

Nick sucked in a deep breath, gathering his thoughts. As he moved to the chair, he scanned each face, smiling and nodding. All in the young and single range, like himself. Some he had met previously, some he hadn't. And Violet, he most definitely had.

"G'day," he said as he sat beside her.

"Oh my goodness, I love your accent." Another voice spoke before Violet had a chance.

Nick dragged his gaze from Violet to where the voice came from. Ah, Willow. He'd met her on Sunday, with her purple hair and hippy clothes. "Um, thanks, I guess." He chuckled self-consciously.

Clare drew everyone's attention. "Since we have a newcomer here tonight, let's all take turns introducing ourselves."

Clare began with herself, and each person took their turn until they got to Violet.

"Well, you've all gotten to know me over the last few months, but what you don't know is I met Nick in Australia last year." She turned to him as different reactions sounded around the room. "May I introduce you? See if I get it right?" She smiled in that way that messed up his thoughts.

"Sure. Why not?" Then again, would this be her chance to dump on him again? Make everyone think he was a villain. No, she wouldn't. They'd sorted it all out, hadn't they?

"This is Nick Gordon. He is from the Northern Territory in Australia. From Jabiru, is it?"

"Actually, a mission station called Oenpeli." He corrected her with a grin. "Not too far away."

"Nick is a skydiving instructor and is here for the summer." She looked at him with a question in her face.

"Yes, that's right."

"How did you meet?" Clare asked.

"Well …" Violet turned to him.

"Go ahead." This would be interesting to hear from her lips. Would this be a story they'd be telling years down the track? Who knew?

"He was our tour guide for the day. I have since learned he isn't a tour guide, although he would make a very good one. He fooled me, that's for sure." She giggled.

Nick watched her. There was no hardness to her words, no

edge to her voice. Perhaps she had let his involvement in her troubles go. "Unintentionally. I love my home, so I can't help but be enthusiastic."

Violet nodded emphatically. "Very enthusiastic."

Everyone laughed.

"On that note, Vi, will you tell us more about your time in Australia?" Clare asked. "You shared some of your testimony on Sunday, but I'm sure there's more."

"I was thinking about it this afternoon. What happened in Australia was really the catalyst that brought to the surface something I've struggled with since childhood."

Clare gave her an encouraging smile. "Go on."

"As I mentioned on Sunday, I've always had trouble with my identity." Violet swallowed and her lips trembled. "Who am I? Why am I here? Is there anything good about me? Those kinds of questions."

Nick felt her pain. Those were common questions, but they hurt just as much for each person.

Violet reached for a tissue and dabbed at her eyes. "Sorry. I can't get through this without getting emotional." She let out a half-laugh. "I cry easily. You'll get to know that about me."

"This is a safe place." Clare rose and came over. Nick relinquished his chair and switched to Clare's now-vacant one. He couldn't be the one to comfort Violet at this time, no matter how much he wished for it. He leaned forward with his elbows on his knees, lowering his head. Watching her hurt was difficult. How had he fallen so hard, so fast?

With Clare rubbing her back, Violet continued. "Anyway, every way I turned, everything I did, I wasn't enough. Even after I came home from Australia, I continued to make mistakes. Not good enough. Not clever enough. Not sensible enough." She sucked in a raw breath. "Now I'm learning that Jesus loves me as I am, but I still find it hard to accept. All those old thoughts keep coming back to plague me."

Clare put an arm tight around her shoulders. "Thanks for being so open with us. And you're right, Jesus does love us as we are. How about we talk about some Bible passages that address this issue?"

It was hard to fathom that someone so beautiful, so refined, so amazing, could have so much doubt about themselves. Nick wanted to tell her how untrue her beliefs were. Instead, he joined in the conversation, using Scripture to say the words. They talked about Psalm 139, how the Lord put everyone together in the womb and knew every intricate detail about each person. Someone even brought up a verse from Song of Solomon. *How beautiful you are, my darling, there is no flaw in you.* Nick smiled to himself. He didn't need the Bible to tell him that about Violet.

At the end of the evening, Violet approached him, all traces of tears gone. Instead, she shared the smile that undid him every time.

"When is your next day off?" she asked. No beating around the bush there.

"Well, I have to mow the grounds of the Bible College on Friday morning, but after that I'm free." Why was she asking?

Violet pulled her phone out and started tapping the screen. "I'll send you my address. Come around and meet my marketing team." Her lips twitched as though amused. "They'd love to hear your ideas for the fundraiser."

"Okay." He drew the word out slowly, not sure what was so funny.

She dropped her phone back into her purse and turned towards the door, but looked back over her shoulder with a flick of her hair that might as well have knocked him in the head for the effect it had on him. "And bring coffee."

CHAPTER SIX

"Why is this I'm hearing about you jumping out of planes?" Violet's father sounded stern down the phone line.

Violet held her breath. This could go either way. "It's for a good cause, Daddy. We're doing a fundraiser for Haven of Hope to help those who work to fight people trafficking." Start with the pacifier.

"We are, are we? Who's we?" He sounded suspicious. Like she'd got in with the wrong crowd or something.

"Me. And I hope you'll be behind me." No sense bringing her friends into this.

A deep sigh sounded through the phone. Violet imagined him running a hand through his hair as he did when exasperated with her. "You couldn't have chosen something safer?"

There it was. He thought she was being reckless again. But she'd done her research. "Daddy, skydiving has a lower rate of injury than many other extreme sports. Look on the internet. And I'm working with a team of high caliber instructors. I'm quite safe."

This would not be a good time to tell him that Nick Gordon,

the man she had accused of deceiving her in Australia, was one of her skydiving instructors. As yet, she hadn't even admitted to Daddy that Nick wasn't responsible for the calamity. She was. Completely. No, he would not be happy. She would keep her mouth shut for now.

"Still …"

Thankfully, he didn't say what she expected him to. *Whatever you're thinking in that head of yours, do the opposite.* That had been his go-to phrase for as long as she could remember.

"I can't say I like it." He sighed again. "Send me everything you've got and I'll check it out. If it all seems sound, I'll back you."

"You will?"

"Of course I will, sweet pea. I just wish you'd come to me first."

Then he would have talked her out of it or directed her to something he deemed more sensible. But no use mentioning that. "Okay. Thanks, Daddy." Violet would just accept the offer.

"And how are things going with Alistair?"

Violet chewed her lip. "Okay, I guess. We haven't seen much of each other. He flies in and out on the weekends, which doesn't give us much time."

"That's the life of a corporate executive."

"I understand." But Violet didn't want to play second fiddle to someone's career the way Mom had always played second fiddle to Daddy's. And as good as Daddy was at what he did, she couldn't help notice Mom often seemed lonely. She didn't want to be like him, like them. "But it means this relationship has to move slowly."

"I can respect that. So no public announcements, then?"

Violet giggled. "Not nearly."

"All right." He chuckled, too. "Love you, sweet pea. Talk to you later."

"Love you too, Daddy." Violet ended the call and made her

way to her home office, where Amelia was working away at a computer.

"The great Morgan Reynolds is ninety percent on board." Violet clapped. "We just need to send him a great proposal."

"Is that all?" Amelia's lips twitched. "Good thing I've been putting one together."

"Of course you have." That's what Violet loved about Amelia —her forethought and initiative.

"I've also locked in a couple of skydivers from an award-winning formation team. They'll help in the last week or so, with choreographing your moves in the air—if that's even the correct term. I've started a crowdfunding event to help generate more donations. We need to work on what happens on the ground. I'm assuming we'll sell tickets?"

"Yes. I'm waiting to hear what Nick has to say, and then we can pull that part together and have something ready for Daddy tonight."

"Nick?"

Violet went to her desk and pretended to rummage through files. "Didn't I tell you? He's coming over later to give us his ideas."

"Hold up. The other day you were mad at him, then you thought he was a stalker."

"Mm-hm." Violet frowned at her diary, turning pages, as if that was where her focus was. "All sorted. It was just a misunderstanding."

Silence for one beat. Two. "Just? That's it? Is there something I need to know?"

Violet rolled her eyes. "Like what? You checked out his story for me. He wasn't to blame for my poor discernment in Australia."

Amelia stared at her, suspicion all over her face. Violet couldn't maintain eye contact and went over to her bookshelf as if she were searching for something. She pulled a book out—it didn't matter which book—and went back to her desk. Amelia continued to stare.

Violet let out a long sigh. "Nick is a friend." A very cute friend with a very cute accent. "And we attend the same church. That common ground is comforting, I find." No lies there. The way the Bible study group had gathered around her and prayed for her meant more than she could say. She'd never experienced support like that. Her usual group of girlfriends all focused on the surface. Exhibit A? They figured a skydiving adventure would fix her funk. Her new church family looked so much deeper. And the fact Nick was one of them? Well, she couldn't ignore him.

"What is with all the church stuff lately, anyway?"

Thankfully, the church topic distracted Amelia from curiosity about Nick. Church she could talk about comfortably. Well, semi-comfortably. "I've been finding answers to many of my questions."

"What kind of questions?"

"Questions about life."

Amelia sat silently, watching her again, but this time Violet offered her a genuine smile.

"Have you become a Christian?"

"Yes, I have, as a matter of fact. And it's the best decision I've ever made. I'd love for you to come along with me sometime and see."

Amelia adjusted her glasses and turned back to her computer screen. "Maybe. But not this Sunday. We're going dancing tomorrow night, remember? It's going to be a late night."

Violet stared at her. "Since when have you been the eager beaver to go dancing?" Amelia was a bookish homebody who usually preferred quiet entertainment, such as reading and watching movies.

Amelia lifted one shoulder in response. "I haven't gotten out much lately."

It sounded like a thin excuse, but Violet left it alone. "Well, I haven't forgotten. Tony's driving us all to Pasco." Violet loved dancing but was no longer sure about the clubbing scene. She didn't want to look like a loser, so she'd agreed to go. It was just a fun night out, dancing with the girls. Nothing more. Did Alistair enjoy dancing? She'd have to ask him when he arrived on Sunday.

And what about …? No, she refused to think about dancing with anyone else. Nick was a friend. That was all.

———

NICK SAT astride the ride-on mower, doing laps of the college's sprawling lawn. The sun beat pleasantly down on his back, without the skin-drenching humidity he was used to back home. His earbuds pumped worship music through his soul and he sang along, losing himself to the stirring melodies and harmonies. This was his happy place. Switched off from the world around him, communing with his Father, heart to heart, through music.

And he needed it. He'd gotten up at six o'clock to call his parents before they went to bed in Australia. They'd spent an hour catching up via a video link. How he missed them. It had only been two weeks, but it felt like a lifetime. He'd never been away from them before. Well, not more than a night or two.

But it had been good to unburden himself a little. They had inevitably asked him how things were going with Violet, and he'd sighed.

"It turns out she has a boyfriend."

"Oh honey." Mum oozed compassion. "That's hard."

"Yeah."

"What are you gonna do now?" Dad asked.

"Well, I guess I have to try keeping my distance." Nick scratched his goatee.

"Sounds wise." Dad nodded. "Why do I sense a but?"

"It's a little difficult. Aside from being one of her skydive instructors, she keeps turning up everywhere I go." Or maybe he was turning up everywhere she went—unintentionally, of course.

"And you really like her, don't you honey?" Mum asked, insightful as ever.

"Yeah, I really do." Then he spent a good fifteen minutes gushing about her, and they were nice enough to listen to every dripping word.

"After today, I'll try to keep our contact limited to skydiving."

"What's happening today?" Dad asked.

"She invited me over this afternoon."

They both gaped and he could see a lecture coming. "Nick —"

"It's a business meeting, okay? I'm meeting with her marketing team to discuss the fundraiser. That's all." Even if it would be nice to see where she lived. He'd heard the houses on the hill were pretty upmarket. "And after that, I'll just ..." Just what? Go to another church? Another Bible study group? The last things he wanted to do when he was just settling in and making new friends.

"Yes? Go on."

"I'll do my best to give her space. I'll try to hang out with Mud more, since he'll be gone in a few weeks."

"That would be a good idea, son," Dad said.

Good idea or no, his heart wanted something totally different. A fact Mum seemed to discern.

"Can we pray with you, honey?" she asked.

"That would be great." He needed all the prayers he could get.

———

THAT AFTERNOON, he pulled his little hatchback into the driveway of a modern two-story house after being buzzed in at the gate. He'd stopped at Becky's coffee cart on the way, but then wondered how many and what particular coffees he was to bring. It would be great if he could remember what Violet ordered last year in Australia, but that was one detail he hadn't seared into his brain. He sent a message to her and received a swift response.

Skinny latte with a shot of caramel for me, and a mochaccino for Amelia.

That was a relief. He'd imagined having to buy and carry coffees for the rest of the team as well and was clueless to how many people that would be.

With the drinks holder in one hand, he pressed the doorbell, which he could see had a camera as well. He turned back to see the view down over the lakes, which shimmered in the sunshine, surrounded by lush greenery. Now, that was a view he could spend hours staring at. A minute later the door opened, and Amelia waved him inside.

"G'day, Amelia."

"Hi, Nick. Come through. We're in the office."

She led him past a living area which presented chic furniture in white and oak with the occasional accent of color. All in tune with what already he knew of Violet.

Inside the office, he looked around, expecting a group of people, but there were none. None save Amelia and Violet, whose sleek office attire knocked him sideways as much as her skydiving suit did. He shouldn't even be here. It wasn't good for him. Not at all.

"Hey, Violet." It came out almost as a gasp. "Where is every-body?" He handed her the latte and gave the mocha to Amelia.

Violet giggled. "I'm sorry, Nick. This time, the deception is mine. Meet my marketing team." She waved her hand toward Amelia, then screwed up her nose in an adorable fashion. "I'm not that grandiose, unfortunately."

"Oh. Right." What an idiot. Heat flushed his face, and he dropped his gaze. Was this deliberate revenge for what he did in Australia? If so, he probably deserved it. He swallowed and looked back up at her, ready to apologize again, but there was a twinkle in her eye. She was just teasing? He chuckled self-consciously. "Yeah. Good one."

"You didn't bring yourself a coffee?" Violet noticed his empty hands.

"Yeah, I'm more of an iced coffee drinker."

"I'm sure Becky sells iced coffee."

"She does, but I have a favorite I can only get at home. It comes in cartons."

"Right." Violet nodded, but he could tell she didn't get it. You couldn't even get his iced coffee in the southern states of Australia, let alone overseas. The Territory's Own it was.

"It's all good. I drank a cola on my way here." Nick gestured toward the floor to ceiling windows that faced over the lakes. "You've got a ripper view out there."

"I'm guessing that means good?" Violet laughed.

Nick gave another self-conscious laugh. "Better than good, but yeah."

"I'm fortunate my father lets me live here." Violet waved toward two sofas which graced the middle of the large office space. "Shall we sit and talk about this fundraiser?"

"Sure." Nick sat on one sofa, while Violet and Amelia sat across from him.

"What did you have in mind?" Violet asked. "I now realize what a huge undertaking this will be, so any ideas are welcome."

"Have you thought about piggybacking off a local air show? There is one running at the airfield where we skydive at the end of summer, if that helps. They'll already have a lot of the planning and marketing underway, which gives you a ready-made audience."

Violet's face lit up. "Amelia, get that down. That is a fantastic idea. Look into that air show and contact the organizers to see if we can be included."

Nick glanced at Amelia to see her scribbling madly with a stylus on her tablet.

"I also thought you could have a giant LED screen and do a live stream of the dive—only for those who make a donation, of course."

"Really? We can do that?" Violet's eyebrows rose.

"I've seen it done. Just need a cameraman or two to jump with you." Nick waved a hand.

"We could ask the professionals to do some extra jumps and do acrobatics in the air." Amelia tapped on her iPad.

"That would be cool," Nick said.

"There might be some space in between dives. We'll need to keep the attendees entertained." Violet said.

"I could probably rustle up some live music for you." Nick had been getting to know some of the church band members. They were quite talented. He reckoned they'd love to be involved.

"So we'll need a stage and sound equipment." Amelia added to her notes.

"You can also use the screen to show video clips about trafficking and how we can help."

"That's good." Violet nodded.

"You could run a sausage sizzle." Sausage sizzles were an essential part of any fundraising effort.

"Sausage sizzle?" Violet's brows rose and Amelia paused in her writing.

"Oh ... like a hot dog stand. In Australia, we can generate thousands by selling sausages, cooked on the barbie ... the grill, and served in a slice of bread with fried onions and tomato sauce … er … ketchup."

They both nodded at him, clearly trying to imagine what he'd described.

"Maybe you could do both a sausage sizzle and a hot dog stand."

"Let's do that." Violet nodded.

"Do you think you'll get up and do a speech before or after your dive, to encourage people to donate?"

"Great idea, now we have a stage." Violet smiled. "Amelia, why don't we contact Haven of Hope and see if they've got a trafficking survivor who is willing to come and share their story?"

"That would be powerful," Nick said as Amelia wrote it down. "This will be an awesome event. I'm really glad to be a part of it."

"It's good to have you on board, Nick." Violet gave him one of those smiles that turned his insides upside down. Yep, he really needed to get some distance from her. It was only a business meeting, yet watching her and listening to her put ideas together made him like her all the more.

Why did she have to have a boyfriend? Seriously. Although, even if she didn't, there was no guarantee she'd feel the same way about him. He groaned inwardly. Why would the Lord bring him all this way just to slam him with a no? Had he been wrong all along? This was doing his head in. Distance was the only answer.

CHAPTER SEVEN

Violet sat in the plane, checking and rechecking, running over the steps in her mind. This was her first unassisted free fall and her adrenaline was peaking. She focused on her breathing, drawing deep breaths, slowing her heart rate. She needed to be cool, calm, clearheaded.

"You'll be fine." Nick winked at her. He must have noticed her tension. Well, given she was opening and closing her hands into fists, it was probably obvious. She shook out her hands and rolled her shoulders.

Of course, Nick would dive alongside her, which was comforting. But she would be on her own. Stabilizing the fall. Pulling the canopy. Guiding her path downward. Landing on the target. It was all up to her. Right now. They were in the drop zone.

Nick raised a fist. "Blue skies."

Violet fist bumped him. "Blue skies."

She moved to the open doorway and sucked in a few more breaths. *Trust me.* Those words whispered through her soul again as she launched out of the plane. Trusting the Lord was a lot like jumping out of a plane and trusting in a parachute. A leap of faith. An exhilarating leap. A beautiful journey. Who knew where the wind could take her? The Lord would guide her just as she could guide and direct the parachute, turning it into the breeze.

Before she knew it, the green grass was speeding to meet her, and she landed close to the target. What a ride. What an experience. She stood there with her eyes closed, head back, drinking in the sensation of having Jesus with her all the way down.

"Are you okay?" Nick jogged up to her. She opened her eyes, although she didn't need to move her head. He was so tall, and his hair looked disheveled after removing his helmet. Why did she even notice these things?

"I'm more than okay, Nick. That was awesome." She pulled off her own helmet and looked back up at him, squinting against the sunshine. "The Lord was speaking to me the whole time."

"Right. That explains the look of euphoria." He helped her pull her canopy in.

"I've never ..." Violet swallowed, the emotion still swelling within.

Nick stopped and looked at her again, a slow smile spreading across his face. "He's good like that, eh?"

All she could do was nod.

"Well, you did great. We can tick that one off as a success. Now we just need to consolidate all your learning through lots of repetition."

"Can't wait."

VIOLET LOOKED FORWARD to dancing at the club with her girlfriends. What a great way to celebrate her achievement in free fall. Laughter filled the drive to Pasco as Breanna and Lilly updated Violet and Amelia on their respective weeks. Breanna was especially vibrant tonight, and Amelia was noticeably quiet in the front seat beside Tony.

"I thought you were excited to come out tonight," Violet leaned forward to whisper in Amelia's ear.

"I am."

"Why so subdued, then?"

"I'm fine. Happy to listen to their stories."

"You're sure?"

"Yes, Vi, I'm sure." Amelia groaned.

The club was pumping with rhythmic bass as they entered, a crush of people bouncing up and down to the beat, arms waving in the air. A hazer filled the space with atmospheric fog, which highlighted blue and pink spotlights that roamed the crowd in time with the music, along with flashes of strobe lighting. Violet had forgotten how loud these places could be.

The four of them joined hands and Breanna led them onto the dance floor, where they whooped and fell in with the writhing mass, singing along to their favorite lyrics. Violet loved to move to music, although this was a far cry from the formality of ballet movements she'd learned as a child. Still, it was great to let her hair down and enjoy the freedom of dance.

Less than half an hour later, a dark mop of curly hair sprung into the middle of their circle.

"Mud?" Violet stopped dancing. What was he doing here?

"Hey, Violet." He hollered the greeting, barely audible over the noise.

Breanna saw her expression and laughed. "Didn't I tell you? Mud's joining us tonight." She moved closer to Mud to dance with him.

Violet turned to Amelia, who looked away, then to Lilly, who gave her a sly wink. They all knew. They'd all said nothing. Why not? It wasn't like she would have objected. She already knew Mud and Bree had hit it off, even though she'd warned Bree to take it easy. Mud would be gone soon, and she didn't want to see her friend get hurt.

Unless …

Unless it had something to do with Nick. She looked over her shoulder. Yes, there he was—at the bar, talking with Tony. Still, it didn't explain why the girls were being so secretive. It's not like there was anything going on between them. She was with Alistair. End of story.

End. Of. Story.

Except she glanced over her shoulder again and saw him coming over. Her heart skipped a beat. Why would it do that? Nick was just a friend.

———

"Go dance with her," Tony told Nick in no uncertain terms. "Otherwise I'll be pulling creeps off her before long."

What was he supposed to say to that? *Sorry, mate. I'm keeping my distance.* Not when there was a danger of some random guy sleazing all over her. No siree. And even without that, Tony was intimidating enough to make Nick say yes to jumping off a cliff. He shoved his hands in the pockets of his jeans as he edged through the crowd to the group of dancing girls … and Mud.

He gritted his teeth. Mud hadn't told him the other girls would be at the club—just Breanna. Mud shouldn't flirt so hard. He'd break the poor girl's heart. For sure, Mud wasn't serious about her. Nick had agreed to be Mud's wingman, mostly to make sure he didn't take it too far.

But now? Now he found himself in the company of Princess Jasmine. Again. The person he intended to avoid as much as possible. But also, the person he wanted to be with. Wow. Violet looked amazing tonight in a cropped yellow blouse with wide sleeves, figure-hugging jeans and strappy heels.

"G'day." He nodded to her and the others. He knew if he

tried to say more, he'd likely trip over his tongue. They waved back, the beat too loud for conversation.

He moved to the music, near Violet, but not too close. This was a bad idea. Too conflicted, on too many levels. He loved music and dancing as much as the next person, but this was not his scene. Nick tried to shake it off as he grooved. The girls were obviously having a great time, and so was Mud. Nick should probably try to enjoy himself.

Less than ten minutes later, Violet let out a "phew" and stopped dancing.

"I'm taking a break." She turned to head for the bar. It took Nick thirty seconds to realize that if Violet wasn't dancing, he didn't need to either. And he should probably stand guard with her at the bar, right? There were plenty of stories of predators spiking girls' drinks. Sure, Tony was watching like a hawk, but what kind of friend would Nick be if he left her alone?

He moved to the bar a couple meters away from where Violet stood, receiving a drink and taking a sip. Nick nodded to the bartender and ordered a soda and lime. When he turned back, Violet was right beside him and his breath caught.

"It seems we run in the same circles now." She leaned closer so he could hear her above the surrounding racket. The silken lengths of her hair brushed his forearm, and he swallowed. So not good.

"So it seems." Even though he was trying to make it otherwise.

The bartender handed him a glass.

"What are you drinking?"

"Nothing exciting. I'm playing Sober Bob tonight." Truth be told, he was always Sober Bob.

"Sober Bob?"

"Designated driver. The person who stays sober and looks out for their mates."

Violet held up her drink of orange juice. "Then I guess I'm

Sober Bob, too. Although Tony's driving." Her eyes lit up as she smiled.

Man, she was cute. He needed to stop looking at her. Nick sipped at his drink and turned to lean against the bar, watching the throng moving in time to the music. Violet did the same, standing close enough that her shoulder bumped his elbow. How was he so aware of her?

"You going back out there?" Please. Please go dance, so he could breathe again.

Surprisingly—happily? Sadly?—Violet shrugged. "I think I've had enough. It was fun, but I'm not sure this is my thing anymore."

Nick nodded. "It's not really my thing either." So now she was going to stand here with him all night? Yikes. He was done for. Doomed.

Unless one of her friends came and dragged her back. He could only hope. His heart could only take so much. Yet his heart was screaming at him for more.

"What are we going to do, then?"

Why would she ask that? Did she even know the suggestions that surged into his head? Heck, all he wanted …

"We could—" *No, Nick. Stop. She has a boyfriend.*

"We could what?"

He could feel her eyes on him, and he shrugged, pretending to focus on finishing his soda.

"I have an idea."

Nick looked down to where she'd just placed a hand on his forearm, sending a shock through his whole body. He surreptitiously moved his arm away. "What's that?"

"We should go find a twenty-four-hour diner where we can have coffee."

No, no, no, no, no. "Sounds great."

"Then let's get out of here."

"What about the others?" Nick jerked his head toward their dancing friends.

"They'll be okay to look after each other for a while." Violet waved Tony over.

Thank goodness for Tony. Of course he would accompany them. Safety in numbers. Being on his own with Violet was the last thing Nick needed. But everything he wanted.

———

CONVERSATION WITH NICK was so easy. Violet just ordered some fries and a hot chocolate, and Nick was downing a full burger meal, which was quite a feat since it was after ten. They laughed and chatted all the while. Should she feel guilty that she enjoyed his company so much? It wasn't like he was doing or saying anything romantic. In fact, apart from that time she thought she heard him propose, there had been no sign he was interested. At all. Perhaps she'd just imagined his proposal.

Yes, they were just friends. Comfortable friends. Too comfortable? Would Alistair be jealous if he knew? Violet glanced aside at Tony, who sat in the booth with them and joined in the conversation over his own late-night snack. Nothing to be jealous about. Violet pushed her doubts aside and focused on Nick.

"Nick, I wanted to ask you something."

"Ask away." His eyebrows rose.

"When did you become a Christian?" She'd been curious for a while. He'd obviously heard her story, but she knew little of his.

A surprised smile lit his eyes. "Great question. Well, I kinda grew up in it. My parents work on a mission station in Arnhem Land, so I learned about the Lord early on. I can't remember not knowing about Him, actually. I probably asked Jesus into my heart as a little tacker. As soon as I could hold a guitar, Dad was teaching me how to play worship songs."

"You play guitar?" Violet picked up another chip. She'd not known that.

"Yeah. A little." He let out that self-conscious laugh that was becoming quite familiar and turned to Tony. "What about you, man? Are you a man of faith?"

Tony swallowed his mouthful and nodded with a wink. "Who do you think took her to the healing services at Easter?"

"Oh, Nick, you should have been there. It was amazing." The memories surged afresh. "This lady told her story about how she received healing from MS. And so many others were healed as well. That's when I realized I needed to take Christianity seriously." It was so refreshing to talk freely about things that were still so new to her, but so precious.

"Sounds awesome." His grin was one hundred percent genuine.

"If you've been a Christian for so long, can you help me with another question?" Violet needed more.

Nick sat up straighter. "Okay. Shoot."

"I've been hearing a lot about God's love for us. But what I want to know is why? Why does he love us? Why would he love us so much he sent his son to die?"

"Ah, the big 'why.'" Nick fiddled with his napkin. "I heard a preacher once say 'because we breathe'. I guess He created us and He loves us because of that—just like anyone loves and takes pride in what they make."

"So why create people who take no notice of Him, who reject Him?"

"You're pulling out the tough questions tonight, aren't you?" Nick chuckled, along with Tony next to him.

"Sorry." Violet dropped her gaze. "I guess I'm wondering why I'm here."

"Don't apologize, Vi. Every question is valid and important."

She liked the way the short version of her name sounded on his lips.

"God created you for a purpose. And I believe God's heart is that everyone comes to Him, even though some don't."

Purpose? She'd never thought of that before. What was her purpose? She held back from asking Nick. She'd try something different.

"So what's your purpose, Nick?"

He shifted in his seat. "Talk about putting me on the spot."

He was uncomfortable. She was pushing too hard. "You don't have to answer if you don't want to."

"It's okay." He took a deep breath and fiddled with the napkin some more. "Finding purpose can be a lifelong journey. I'm still working it out. I know I'm here to serve the Lord, but in the last couple of years, I've just been grateful to be alive."

What? Violet became more alert and Tony's head swiveled to look straight at Nick. "What do you mean by that?"

"Well, I'm an electrician by trade —"

"Wait. What?" More surprises.

"I'm a qualified electrician, but it didn't make sense to retrain here for only a few months."

That seemed reasonable. Even though the thought of him leaving again felt like being dosed with a bucket of cold water.

"A couple years ago I was working on high voltage wires. I didn't know a cable was live. I was electrocuted and thrown clear. The doctors reckon the jolt stopped my heart, but the way I landed gave me a kick start. Broke a few ribs, though. It's a miracle I survived."

Both she and Tony stared at him with open mouths.

"Although it's weird. Sometimes, you can still feel electricity zinging through my hands." He reached out his hand. "Touch my thumb."

Violet hesitantly reached out, still mesmerized by the story. She put a finger on his thumb and—

"Boo!"

Violet shrieked. Then laughed. Then slapped his arm. Even Tony doubled over, laughing.

"Do you do that to everyone?"

Nick put his hands up in surrender, although his shoulders shook with silent laughter. "Guilty."

———

"Is it true?" Violet looked at him with narrowed eyes. Clearly, she still thought of him as capable of deception. Pranks, yes. Outright lies, no.

"The electrocution is. Here," he pulled out his phone, opened the photo gallery and scrolled before turning it toward her to show photos of him in the hospital with a heart monitor and other machines attached.

"That's incredible Nick. And you survived."

"Yep. God is good." The recovery wasn't much fun, but he was all good now and loving life.

Violet didn't hand back his phone. Instead she tapped away on the screen. What was she doing?

"Tell me about Nicky Ned," she said with a twitch of her lips, still playing with his phone.

"Oh, that." Heat rose in his neck. Did he really have to tell her? They would both laugh at him now. He cleared his throat. "When I was in high school, probably what you would call your freshman year, I started to take a firm stance on outworking my Christian morals, I guess. The guys—Mud and the rest of my friends—would try to make me swear, or shoplift something small, or smoke, drink, whatever. When I kept refusing every-thing, they ended up calling me Ned Flanders after the char-acter from The Simpsons."

They were both laughing before he even finished.

"That's hilarious," Violet said.

"I thought I'd outgrown it, but Mud set up my social profile a year ago and that's what he put for my name. I don't know how to change it." Shame on him. He'd been super slow catching up with technology, but that's what he got, growing up in a remote community with little connectivity to the outside world.

"And the Shrek avatar?"

Nick gritted his teeth. "Mud again. Calls me big and ugly, and do you remember my green four-wheel drive?"

She stared at him. Was that sympathy in her eyes? She opened her mouth, closed it again, but finally spoke. "I can fix it for you, if you like."

Since she still had his phone in her grasp, he shrugged. "Sure."

She tapped on his phone and held it up. "Smile." She took a photo, tapped some more, and handed his phone back. "There. All done."

"Hey, you two." Tony, who had been mostly quiet, straightened. "It's after one. The club will close soon. We should get back."

Nick glanced at his phone. Heck. Where had the time gone? Hours had disappeared while he chatted to Violet, and he didn't feel in the least sleepy. He grabbed his jacket and followed them out the door. This couldn't be good for him, couldn't be good for his heart. He was so drawn to her. If he kept spending time with her, it was going to start hurting real soon. Distance. He needed distance.

The next morning, he dragged himself out of bed after a scant four hours' sleep, ready to go to church. A church where he would likely see Violet Reynolds again. Everything within him wanted to be near her, but he would keep his distance. He would.

He hummed worship songs as he showered and sang as he threw bread in the toaster, while the Franklins teased him.

"Look what the cat dragged in," Lexi laughed.

Did he appear that tired? He didn't feel it. He was still buzzing from the conversation with Violet last night.

Nick whistled as he locked his car and strode toward the front doors of the church.

"Morning, Nick." A voice captured his attention from the side. He turned. Tony stood with his back leaning against the Mercedes he drove Violet around in.

"G'day, Tony." Was Violet inside waiting to speak to him again?

"Can I have a word with you?"

Not Violet then. "Sure." He walked over to Tony. "What's up?"

Tony folded his arms across his chest. Big arms, too, they were. Funny, Nick had never felt truly intimidated by this man, until now. Something in his expression …

"I'm going to need you to back off."

Nick stiffened. What? "Is something wrong?"

"Yeah. People are talking about you. They're calling you a gold digger. I just heard two women talking this morning. They didn't know I was there."

Sucker punch. What? How? Who even? And why? He was practically a stranger to everyone. "I don't understand."

"They are saying you're only here for Violet and that must be because she's an heiress."

"Seriously?" Nick winced. *Precious.* Only a handful of people knew he'd come to America for Violet, though not because of money. Never that. He hadn't even known she was an heiress, as Tony put it. So where did the rumors come from? Mud. Of course. Not that it was anyone's business.

"So I need you to stay away from her. It's not personal. It's my job to protect her. She's a good girl, and she doesn't need to be caught up in some town scandal."

Anger roiled. It was completely unfair. He wanted to argue, wanted to defend himself. He'd done nothing to hurt Violet.

Would never. And therefore, he must listen to Tony. He must swallow his pride, and his desire to be near her. Why did people have to be so awful?

"Fine." Nick gritted the word out and swiveled to go back to his car.

"For what it's worth," Tony called out behind him. "I don't believe you're a gold digger."

Nick spun back to him, shoving down his frustration. "Thanks, I guess. But can I ask you something?"

"Sure."

"Why does she need protection? Is it just that, to stop gold diggers as you call them?"

Tony pushed away from the car, his brows furrowing. "Partly. She would call me a chaperone. Her father would call me security." He sighed. "Look, Violet rarely sees the bad in people—"

"I would not call that a fault."

"Neither would I. However, it has landed her in hot water more than once. A potentially serious incident at college led Mr. Reynolds to hire me."

"What happened?" Nick's stomach did a little flip of concern. "If you don't mind me asking."

"Some young guys thought it would be a great prank to pretend to kidnap her for ransom. You'll have to hear the rest from her. It's not my place. Needless to say, it worried her father enough to hire me."

Nick nodded, though his irritation rose again. "Right. And now you're shielding her from me and gossip. I get it." He swung around and continued to his car.

"Like I said, it's not personal." Tony called after him.

CHAPTER EIGHT

Violet sat in the car with Alistair, who was driving her to Walla Walla for lunch and a tour of a local vineyard. She appreciated the romantic nature of this date. This might be a good time to connect on a deeper level, while he was busy at the wheel and not distracted by his phone. See if they could have an easy and in-depth conversation like she'd had with Nick. Not that she was comparing. Of course not. But if this was the man she was supposed to end up marrying, they should be able to talk.

"How has your week been?" she asked.

"Very busy." He shifted his grip on the steering wheel glancing at her. "I've basically been in meetings all week. Finance department, legal department, logistics, IT, sales and marketing, you name it. With this merger coming up, there is an exceptional amount to be across."

Even now, his phone was pinging every few seconds. He kept looking down at the cell, clearly wanting to check the messages. Instead, he launched into an explanation of how the merger was progressing. Dry data and formulaic strategies.

Violet understood it all, having studied business, but her interest waned. She wanted to know more about him than about his career. She stared at his handsome profile. His expressions as he discussed business were enthusiastic, to say the least.

When he paused, she dropped in a change of subject. "Tell me what you like to do outside of work."

"What do you mean?" He shifted his grip again.

"Hobbies. That kind of thing. For instance, do you enjoy dancing?"

"Yes." The word was drawn out, as though he was unsure. "Remember, I am coming with you to the gala dinner-dance for the homeless youth thing in a few weeks."

That didn't really answer her question. "What about hiking? Fishing? Swimming? Sport? What do you do in your downtime?"

"I haven't done much of that, but sometimes I get into board games with friends, and I've done a few cooking classes. Is that what you mean?"

"Yes." Now they were onto something. "What can you cook? Perhaps you can make me dinner sometime?"

"All right. How about you come to Seattle next weekend, and we can try that? But I'm not telling you what I'm making. It will be a surprise." He looked across at her and his lips curved upward.

Yeah, okay, he had an attractive smile. She leaned back and looked out the windows, enjoying the scenery. It was a beautiful area. She didn't understand why Daddy and Alistair loved being in the city so much. Violet loved the wide-open spaces, the outdoors, the clean air.

They soon pulled into the vineyard, and Violet jumped out of the car to admire the rows of vines stretching in every direction from where she stood.

"I'll just be a minute," Alistair called from inside the car. How much time would he spend checking his messages? Answering even one could lead him on a tangent for half an hour or more. Funny. She flashed back to the evening before. Nick hadn't touched his phone once until he showed her the photos of his hospital stay. Violet liked that. She didn't want technology to take away from the enjoyment of the moment. Technology had its place. But that place was not during a date. Not that she'd been on a date with Nick or anything. This was a date though, yet Alistair struggled to let his work go, even for a short time.

Violet sighed and leaned against the car. She might as well check her own phone. Nothing interesting there. Nothing that couldn't wait until tomorrow, anyway. And no message from Nick. She chewed her lip. When she held his phone last night, she'd sent a message to herself, and then replied to it early this morning just before going to bed. She'd wanted him to have her personal number, so he didn't have to keep contacting her through her social pages. Why did she want him to contact her, anyway? With a grunt, she shut the phone off and dropped it into her purse.

———

"Who did you tell, Mud?" Nick challenged his friend as soon as Mud opened the door to his cabin. Nick had stewed throughout the service at Trinity Life Church. He probably shouldn't have gone there at all in his current attitude.

"Tell what?" Mud ran a hand through scruffy hair. He'd clearly just gotten out of bed. Leaving the door open, he turned and flopped down on the sofa.

"That I came here for Violet?"

Mud yawned. "Only Bree. Why?"

"Great. Just Great." Nick sank onto one of the remaining chairs. Why couldn't Mud stay quiet? "I'm guessing she's told others, because the rumor spreading around town is that I'm only after Violet's money. And now her security guy has told me to stay away." Even though he'd already decided that's what he had to do.

"No way." Mud sat up straight. "Dude, that sucks. I'm sorry. I didn't know that would happen. How rich is this chick?"

Nick shrugged. "I'm guessing she's wealthier than I thought."

"Can I make it up to you? Is there something I can do?" Mud seemed genuinely sorry.

"Other than deny any rumors you hear, not much. I'm going to have to lay low for a while."

"Sorry, man. I didn't think." A common problem with Mud. "I guess that means we can hang out more, though. I'll call off my plans with Bree tonight."

True to his word, Mud canceled his date with Bree and made very few new dates with her. Nick spent all his spare time with Mud, trying to keep his thoughts away from Princess Jasmine. Except for that text message on his phone. He hadn't seen it until Sunday night. *I wanted you to have my personal number. Call me.*

It felt like a hundred times a day he went to type a reply or call her, then deleted or canceled. Tony's words kept ringing through his head. He had to do the right thing, including changing his shifts at the skydiving center, so they didn't clash with Violet's training sessions. But, oh, how he missed her already. As if missing Arnhem Land and his family wasn't enough.

———

TWO WEEKS PASSED and Nick seemed to have vanished from Violet's life. He hadn't shown up at church, or the bible study. She hadn't even seen him at Freefall Adventures. It seemed strange. But he was only here for the summer, so she shouldn't worry about it. She tried to shrug off the pangs of loss left in his wake. She shouldn't feel attached to him at all.

Especially since Bree had told her something Mud had mentioned. That Nick had come to America solely to meet her again. A piece of information that both flattered and confused her. If it was true, he'd gone to a lot of trouble for her. That was huge. But was it true? It wasn't like Nick had made any moves on her. She hadn't seen him for two weeks, and he had even stopped commenting on her social pages. Was something wrong? Had he changed his mind? Not that it should matter.

Besides, things were improving with Alistair. She'd had a lovely weekend with him in Seattle, as well as spending time with Daddy and Mom. Alistair had cooked her some French cuisine, impressing her with his skills in the kitchen. He'd turned on soft jazz music and they'd danced together in the living room. It had been romantic and lovely, until his hands started moving around her back, pulling her close and his head dipped towards hers.

Violet's nerves had kicked into gear, and she'd backed away quickly. She'd never been in that situation before and wasn't ready.

"What's wrong, Violet?" Alistair had asked, brows furrowed.

"Um …" She'd scrambled for an excuse. "It's getting late. I should probably head back to Mom and Daddy's."

"Come on, babe." Alistair's voice almost sounded whiny. "I was only going to kiss you."

Her heart fluttered. With what? Anticipation? No, more like insecurity. She'd never thought of kissing anyone except Lyall. Why should Alistair's intention surprise her? At that moment, she didn't know. Alistair was attractive to look at, and pleasant to be around, but did she want to make it official? No, she wasn't ready. Not sure enough about him to go further. "I'd rather get to know you more first. Is that okay?"

Thankfully, he'd let her go without further pressure, and the next evening, he'd taken her to the ballet. Watching men and women twirl around on the stage stirred up old dreams. She'd once aspired to be a professional dancer, and her tutors thought she had the talent to pursue ballet. Unfortunately, Daddy considered it a frivolous pursuit and convinced her to follow him into business.

Sometimes she wished her parents had another child, a son, someone who loved the executive world as much as Daddy did. But she was the only child, so she allowed Daddy to mold her as he saw fit. She'd never been able to convince him she couldn't be, couldn't do all he expected of her. He seemed so proud of her imagined success, like he was blinded to reality. Except for every time she made too-impulsive decisions that caused problems for his company. Then, perhaps, for a moment, he saw the truth. Soon enough, though, he tried to fix her again.

The trouble was, every time she went to Seattle, Daddy put the pressure on her to move back there. It was subtle pressure, but it was there. And now Alistair did the same. They insisted if she didn't live so far away, they could spend more time together. Which was obvious. But the concrete jungle sapped her energy —something they could not, or would not, understand. Besides, she needed space from Daddy's constant micromanaging, something he would flat-out deny should she challenge him.

And these days, Violet felt uncomfortable in her own skin. Didn't really understand who she was. And purpose? Nick had talked about purpose. She had no idea. That God called her a beloved daughter was a starting point, she supposed. She needed to read more of what God said about her in the Bible. Was she meant to be in this role with Daddy's company? Or was she made for something else? It was a question that came to her often.

Violet brushed those deep thoughts aside. Today was Independence Day and tonight she and her friends were going to Lake Wainscott to swim, eat and watch the Fourth of July fireworks from the lakefront. It was a Thursday night, so Alistair couldn't join her. Something about a late business meeting, he'd said, hinting that if she was in Seattle, they could have caught late fireworks together somewhere.

Violet sighed as she collected her bag and met Tony at the car. She would enjoy a night of celebration with her girlfriends in this beautiful town she loved. She'd arranged to meet the girls near the stone bridge. From there, they'd walk along the lakefront to find a suitable spot to sit.

When Tony pulled up, the girls were already waiting for her. "I'll find a park and catch up with you," he said as she got out.

"No problem." She waved and headed for her friends.

"Let's go for a swim first, before the temperature drops too much," Lilly suggested as soon as they'd greeted each other. They hurried to where a merry crowd was already in the water, laughing and splashing.

It wasn't till after they'd had a quick dip and changed back into dry clothes that they walked along the lakefront, searching for a good vantage point for the fireworks. They wouldn't be until much later, but more and more people were arriving by the minute.

Then Violet spied him—them—sitting on picnic blankets closer to the water. Nick, along with the Franklins and several other church people, all in one area.

"Here." Violet dropped her bag and laid out a picnic rug. "This looks like the perfect spot." None of the girls had recognized Nick from behind.

"There you are." Tony jogged up.

"Sorry. We went for a swim first."

Tony scoured the area and raised his eyebrows when he turned back to her. Yes, he'd seen Nick. But the people he was with were their church family, too. Tony said nothing, just made himself comfortable on the grass.

Soon her friends all stretched out, lying on the grass, basking in the afternoon sunshine, except Bree, who went to buy them all sodas.

It wasn't long before the rhythmic sound of a guitar rang out, and the church group began singing praise songs. As Violet looked over at them, she realized it was Nick playing the guitar, and his voice was prominent among them. Wow. And he could sing.

———

NICK SAT on the picnic blanket, strumming the guitar. Peter had handed him the instrument out of the blue and told him to lead them in a couple of songs. No problem there. He didn't need an excuse to worship. Anywhere. Anytime.

Lyn and others from church had packed an enormous picnic hamper, and there was a big spread of food laid out. It reminded him of big family get togethers at home. Laughing, eating, singing, telling silly stories, laughing some more. With his three sisters and all the extended family, each time they gathered was like a big party. This felt the same, although most of the faces were still unfamiliar. As he watched them, he wondered which of them might have spread rumors about him. Sadness lingered that people would do such a thing.

And around him, couples snuggled together in the fading light in every direction he looked. Lexi and Jackson, and Matt and Ari, who was out of her wheelchair and leaning against Matt on the blanket. Even Peter and Lyn were cozying up and holding hands, which reminded him of his parents and how much he missed them. It would be a romantic evening if he weren't alone. Not even Mud was with him tonight. He'd volunteered to take some night divers on tandem jumps to see the fireworks from above. Well, at a safe distance.

Nick picked up the guitar and wandered down to the water's edge, where he could be alone with his sullen thoughts. He sat and began picking at strings while watching the sun set in the west, the colorful hues reflected from the rippling lake water. Beautiful. Soothing. Just what he needed.

Lord, I thought you were in this.

Silence. Nick continued to brood, playing a wistful tune on the guitar. Had he been all wrong? From the beginning? Should he pack up and go home? His family would fill this hole in his heart with their love and dependable support. He missed them more than he had expected.

"Hey." Someone plopped down beside him. "Are you ghosting me now?"

Violet. Nick's heart got up and did a lap around his whole body, then screamed to a halt, his fingers suddenly finding all the wrong strings on the guitar. How to answer her? Yes, he was ghosting her. Not because he wanted to. Because he had to. But he couldn't say that without telling her everything. "I ... uh ..." He shifted the guitar to the grass beside him and swiveled to see where Tony was. Ah yes, watching from back there, a stern look on his face.

"No, no. Keep playing. I was enjoying it." Violet put a hand on his forearm, sending electricity through him. Thankfully, she pulled it away again as he reached for the acoustic.

He began plucking the strings again, wracking his brain for something acceptable to say and finding nothing.

"I thought you said you could only play a little." Violet nudged him with her elbow.

Nick chuckled, self-conscious at her implied compliment. What was he going to say?

"So ..." Violet dragged the word out after a long silence. "Bree told me something that Mud told her."

Discordant notes filled the air as his fingers stumbled again, his subconscious confirmation of the gossip.

"Is it true?"

As if he hadn't given it away by blundering on the guitar.

And his playing wasn't getting any better, his fingers suddenly slick with anxiety. He stopped strumming but held the instrument in his lap. He swallowed the ball of fear in his throat. Honesty time. "Yeah, it's true." He took a breath and shook his head. "But not the fortune-hunter part."

"What fortune-hunter part?"

She hadn't heard that bit? Precious. Now he'd spread the town gossip himself. Nick gritted his teeth. "That's what people are saying about me."

Violet gasped and put her hand over her mouth. "Oh, no. Really?"

"Truth is, I didn't know you were the daughter of a bigwig tycoon." Nick blew out a long breath. "All I saw was a fun and gorgeous girl, a girl I wanted to get to know better." He shrugged as he finished.

Her hand shifted from her mouth to her heart. "Oh Nick. I'm so sorry."

Nick dared to turn and make eye contact. The force of his attraction slammed him in the chest once again and his breath caught. Oh, how he wished ...

Violet's eyes drifted to his lips momentarily, but then she coughed and turned her focus to the lake, where sparkling lights reflected from the shimmering water. "I live under certain expectations. My father will hand his empire over to me one day, and he wants me to have a partner who can run it with me."

Nick nodded. Of course he did. An invisible hand squeezed his heart, strangling it. Why did he ever come here? All this way, to fall so hard, and for what? Nothing.

"Nick..." Her hand was on his forearm again and he couldn't breathe. "That you came all the way to America is an enormous compliment. It means more to me than I can say. But I can't offer you anything more than friendship." She leaned forward to make direct eye contact with him. "I would really appreciate that friendship."

How could he say no to that beautiful face? Even though friendship would be a painful exercise. He lifted the corners of his mouth in an attempt at a smile and raised a fist. "Friends."

Violet knocked his fist with her own. "Good. Now, will you come and join the rest of us? The fireworks are about to start."

CHAPTER NINE

A week later, Mud grabbed Nick by the arm as they exited the hangar one afternoon. "Hey dude, I've got a great idea."

Oh no. That couldn't be good. Mud was always up to some prank or other. "Right. What great idea is that?"

"A double date. Me and Bree, you and Vi." Mud almost skipped beside him as they walked to their car. Well, Mud almost needed to take two steps for each one of his. But wait. Double date? Nick rolled his eyes.

"Man, you know there is nothing happening there. Why would you even suggest it?"

Nick was still keeping his distance from Violet, although they had chatted a little via text messages, mostly her figuring out questions about her new faith. He loved being able to talk her through those issues.

"Nah, but we won't call it a date. You know it would be good for Violet to dive into a different drop zone. You can sign off on it in her logbook and call it part of her training. The fact that we stop at a scenic picnic spot on the way back has nothing to do with it." But the grin on Mud's face, along with his wiggling eyebrows, said otherwise.

Nick shook his head, laughing. "You sly dog." The idea sparked interest in him, although nothing would come of it. "Violet will never go for it."

Mud bounced in front of him, slapped him on the shoulder, then walked backwards. "That's where you're wrong. She's already said yes."

Nick stopped dead in his tracks. "What? How?" Tony would never have agreed. Somehow Mud—or Violet—must have convinced him it would be fine.

"Come on, man. This is my last week. We need to do something fun, one last escapade before I go home." Mud pulled up the maps on his phone. "See, we drive out to Prosser. Tony will meet us there with the girls. Then we'll stop at one of these parks on the Columbia River on the way back. We'll fire up the barbie—the grill, have a delicious lunch, then walk the trail along the river here, before we all drive back."

Mud was some kind of magician. He'd got Tony not just to agree, but to come along. Which actually made complete sense. Nick sighed. "All right. I'm in." Although this couldn't be good for his heart.

VIOLET COULDN'T STOP THINKING about the fact that Nick had come to America just for her. Just for her. No one had ever gone to that much trouble for her. Ever. And it wasn't like he was rolling in cash like many people in her circle were. He must have saved for a while to get here. Did he like her that much?

She couldn't help reading and rereading her journal of that day with him in Australia. She couldn't deny it. There had been an attraction from the start for her as well. But it couldn't amount to anything. Daddy would never buy it. And then there was Alistair, Daddy's choice. If only she had the freedom to make her own choices.

Whatever is in your head, do the opposite.

Right. She couldn't trust her own feelings and impulses. She needed to remember that. Especially today on this skydive practice-slash-picnic. They were just friends.

Yet her breath left her when he smiled down at her on arrival at the airport in Prosser.

"All set?"

"Yes." Pity they weren't doing tandem dives anymore. Violet groaned internally. Where had that thought come from? She shook off the fluttering threatening to take over.

"Woo-hoo. Let's do this." Mud came charging out of the hangar, greeted Bree by swinging her around in the air, took her hand and ran back to the hangar for their chutes.

"Look who's an eager beaver." Violet twitched her lips wryly.

"Yeah. Nothing but full throttle for Mud." Nick strolled beside her to go inside and prepare for their jump.

Minutes later, they were on the plane, heading up into the blue yonder. When they reached the drop zone, Nick waved her over to the open door.

"Have a look down and get your bearings. You're aiming for a different landing spot than usual," he yelled above the noise of the plane.

"Okay."

"Our target is that area of grass at the airport. Do you see it?"

"I see it."

"All right. Let's go then. Blue skies."

With those words, he dropped backward out of the Cessna into free-fall. Violet admired him somersaulting for a moment before she followed suit. She'd learned some acrobatics over the last few weeks but wasn't as adventurous as Nick. Not yet.

She kept him in view, along with Mud and Bree above her, also keeping track of where their landing target was. Once she released the canopy, then it was a matter of adjusting and turning until she landed safely right where Nick had showed her. Well, close enough.

The four of them gathered their parachutes in, packed them away and headed for the cars to drive to the picnic spot, where they discovered a surprise. Amelia and Lilly were waiting for them. Violet couldn't help but wonder who had included them. Had Mud invited them? Or Bree or Nick? Maybe it was Tony. There was no way to know without asking, but it didn't matter. She was happy to see them there.

They worked together to lay a table under a shelter and unpack the food. The guys had the grill sizzling with meat and onions, making her mouth water.

"Suddenly, I'm famished." She laughed as Tony handed her a backpack. A change of clothes.

"Smells amazing," Nick agreed.

"Let's eat, then." Mud was ready to jump in.

"I'm going to get out of this jump suit first." Violet nodded toward the rough bathroom in the distance. She was the only one who'd worn a jump suit today. The others jumped in their shorts and tees, or in Bree's case, Lycra and tee covered by a hoodie which she'd now removed.

The seven of them tucked into sticky ribs, steak, grilled corn, and salad, while laughing at Mud and Nick's antics.

Nick stole a rib from Mud's plate when he wasn't looking. On discovering the missing food, Mud launched into a hilarious string of threats, spoken in a French accent with excessive dramatic flair. How he kept a straight face, Violet had no idea.

"Zees is an affront to my magnifique, 'ow you say, personality. *En garde*, sir." Mud brandished a stick of carrot like a sword.

Nick collected a paper straw, held it aloft, and rose to face him—well, tower over him, his face as grim as if Mud held an actual sword and declared the superiority of his "knife."

Amelia squealed and hurriedly whispered in Violet's ear.

"That was a line from *Crocodile Dundee*." This was right up Amelia's alley. She'd been a movie buff for as long as Violet had known her.

Nick and Mud set to it, fighting with their "weapons," quoting lines of various movies in funny voices, to the hilarious laughter of the rest of them. Amelia named each movie of their inane argument between giggles. Nick soon had Mud on the ground, his straw at Mud's throat.

Violet looked at Amelia, a little lost. None of it made sense to her. Words about poets and peanuts, which the other girls quoted in unison.

"From *The Princess Bride*," Amelia told her.

Oh, yes, that was one movie she'd seen, although she couldn't remember all the lines as everyone else seemed to.

Bree had almost choked on her corn and Lilly was gripping her sides, while Amelia wiped tears of laughter from her eyes. Even Tony's frame was shaking as he tried to keep from snorting. Violet couldn't remember cackling so much in years. Well, except for that day last year in Australia with Nick.

The rest of the afternoon passed with more laughter, the boys continuing to spar on and off for any imagined and ridiculous offense. And on their walk, Mud turned all David Attenborough, mimicking his accent as he explained a rock on the side of the path, or a blade of grass, or the water that trickled by in the river. Nick kept him going, of course, asking questions about nonsensical things.

Violet closed her eyes on the drive home, feigning sleep. She didn't want to talk. She just wanted to relive every moment of the day. What a fun day it had been. The best. She was even a little sad to know Mud would head back to Australia in a few days. How sad would she be when Nick left? It didn't bear thinking about. Until then, she would just enjoy his company.

———

"THIS IS NOT A GOOD IDEA," Tony told Violet, his mouth set in a grim line.

Violet dropped her gaze to the floor. Why had she even mentioned it? Alistair had called last night and said he couldn't join her for the gala dinner-dance. Some important business meeting had come up, and he wouldn't be able to get away in time. But she had two tickets and didn't want to waste them.

"Why not? Those tickets cost a lot of money." But the truth had nothing to do with the cost. The money was going toward a good cause, after all. She wanted to ask Nick to take the other ticket and had inadvertently blurted that desire out in front of Tony.

"Because he likes you, that's why." Tony's reply was exactly what she knew he'd say.

Violet sighed and folded her arms across her chest. "Nick and I have talked about this. We have an understanding. We're just friends. Besides, he's going back to Australia in a few weeks. Nothing's going to happen."

"You like him too, don't you?" Tony stared at her until she had to look away.

Violet groaned. "We're just friends." When Tony said nothing, just stood there and watched her, she crumbled. "Fine. Yes. A little."

"And what about Alistair?"

"What about him?" Violet rubbed her arms, though she wasn't cold. Tony merely raised his eyebrows at her.

"I'm not sure he's the one for me."

Tony drew in a long breath and let it out slowly. "I may be out of line, but I agree with you."

Violet's gaze snapped to his. *What?*

"But you can't go toying with either of their affections, Violet. You need to decide." He gave her arm a squeeze and walked away, leaving her in thought.

She wasn't toying with anyone, was she? She had made no

promises to either man. The only thing she'd committed to was seeing Alistair, for Daddy's sake. After Lyall, she wasn't in a hurry to throw her hopes in any direction.

Whatever is in your head, do the opposite.

Not this time, Daddy.

———

PRECIOUS LORD. Why on earth had Nick agreed to this? Now he was sitting in the Mercedes with Violet and Tony, whose face appeared sour to say the least, for a two-plus hour drive to Spokane. Thankfully, Violet had taken the front seat, putting a little distance between them. He couldn't see her face, which would only increase the palpitations his heart threw every five minutes.

A dinner-dance with Violet. What could be wrong? Although Nick knew he was putting his heart in dangerous territory, he couldn't find it in himself to say no. Considering he wasn't sure how long he'd stay, this could be his last opportunity to spend any real time with Violet.

He'd said goodbye to Mud a few days ago, driving him to the airport, and now he was on his own. And the question had arisen again—was it worth him staying on if there was truly no hope? Had he wasted all this effort on a fantasy? Because, face it, that's what everyone around him seemed to think. Including Mud, who'd probably got the inside information from Bree and the others.

But now, he was almost in Spokane, with Violet. It was going to be a long day-slash-night as Tony had insisted they weren't to stay over in Spokane, despite the distance. He was becoming like the overbearing parent of teenagers. Seriously.

"Do you have a tux?" Violet had asked him over the phone, after he agreed to be her plus-one.

"Absolutely," he'd grinned. "I packed several in my suitcase for such an occasion."

He enjoyed the tinkle of laughter that came through the phone.

"Then I'm going to have to take you shopping, Mr. Australia. Can you cope?"

"What's the shopping like in Spokane? I love a good bargain."

Silence for a second. Two. "Are you being sarcastic again?"

"No, actually." He chuckled. "I love shopping. It will have to be a rental tux, though. I'm not that flush."

He held his breath, hoping she wouldn't insist on buying one for him.

"If you can cope with shopping, I can cope with a rental."

So now they were on their way. They'd left quite early to book the tux in and give them time for any adjustments to be made during the day while they continued with other shopping. He needed dress shoes, of course, and Violet would be at a hair stylist after lunch. Other than that, they could just browse and hang out.

And hanging out with Violet was the absolute best. As they strolled through the mall, his fingers knew an itch to hold her hand. Oh, what would that be like? Just having her near was a rush similar to falling out of a plane.

"Let's go in here." Violet pointed to a discount bargain shop.

Not what he expected. He thought she'd aim for all the high-end stores. Maybe she was saying it just for him. "Sure." He followed her.

"Sometimes I find cute things in these stores," she said.

Okay, so not just for him. "Lead the way." He tried to gesture, but several shopping bags weighed his arm down. Tony had offered to carry them, but Nick insisted on bearing his own burdens. As he'd hoped, he'd found a few bargains aside from the dress shoes. His stomach growled, though. It must be nearly time for lunch.

———

"Aw, LOOK AT THIS," Violet held up a tiny porcelain rabbit with enormous eyes and drooping ears. It held a yellow sunflower.

Nick looked over at her and his lips curved up. "Adorable." Did he mean the knick-knack, or something more? *Stop it, Violet.* She shouldn't be hoping for more.

She watched him surreptitiously from the corner of her eye. He was tapping his feet and humming as he browsed. Actually, more than his feet that were moving to the music. Violet tuned into the store's background music. *Footloose.* This could be fun.

Violet picked up a candlestick, stepped toward Nick, and lip-synced into the stick like it was a microphone.

Without missing a beat, Nick grabbed the nearest thing at hand, a small vase, and joined her, his face spread with a wide grin. They danced around each other, mouthing the words, while Tony looked on, shaking his head.

When the song finally ended, a couple of people in the vicinity clapped. Goodness. She hadn't realized anyone was watching. Heat flooded her face as she dropped her forehead against Nick's laughing chest, attempting to hide her blush. A subtle movement from him shocked her back into reality. What was she doing? She backed away from him.

"Sorry, Nick."

A glance toward Tony revealed his scowling face staring back at her. At them. Violet bit down on her lip. She was supposed to be living up to her word that she and Nick were just friends. And then she did stupid things like that? Tony would never believe her again.

"All good." Nick took the candlestick from her and replaced the items on the shelf. "Time for food?"

"Yes, let's go eat." Violet hurried out of the store and headed for the food court, Tony on her heels.

But it was a minute before Nick caught up to her.

"You forgot this." He held up the little rabbit she'd admired.

"You didn't have to do that."

Nick merely shrugged, shifting his gaze to the food options. "What are you having? My shout."

"Your shout?" Violet was lost.

"Oh, we say that in Australia. It means I'm buying. That goes for you too, Tony."

"Right. Thank you. I think I'd like sushi," Violet said.

"Appreciated." Tony asked for fried chicken.

Nick bought the food, and they sat at a table and laughed over their *Footloose* fiasco. Time disappeared too quickly. Violet was due at the hair stylist soon, then Tony would take Nick to collect his suit.

On their way out of the mall, Nick stopped to buy more food. Violet couldn't believe he was still hungry after a big lunch like that, although it seemed quite common with young men. However, as they stepped outside, Nick approached a homeless man who sat nearby and handed him the meal.

Violet stopped in her tracks. Something about that act of kindness triggered her, a ball rising in her throat.

"What's the matter?" Nick asked as he returned.

Violet swallowed. "Why did you do that?"

He shrugged. "I figured he was hungry. I saw him on the way in. Least I can do."

Violet had seen the man on the way in also and had felt sorry for him. But her father's voice was ever in her head. *Do the opposite*. What if the opposite was the wrong thing to do? What if the opposite was holding her back?

"Have I done something wrong?" A concerned frown drew Nick's brows together.

"No, no." Violet shook herself free of her troubling thoughts and wiped at a tear that leaked from her eye. "That was a lovely thing to do."

Quite perfect, actually. Nick was quite perfect. Forget the

friends thing. She wanted more, and she couldn't deny it. But that didn't mean more would work. Violet shook her head again and headed for the car where Tony waited.

God, please take this attraction from me if it's not meant to be.

Of course it wasn't. It was just a silly crush because he'd come across the world for her. These feelings would fade away soon.

Surely.

CHAPTER TEN

The evening had arrived. Nick showered and dressed in one room of the resort suite Violet had booked for the day. He looked around the luxurious room again. Pity they wouldn't be staying overnight. He could enjoy this indulgence, even if only once in his lifetime.

Nick waited with Tony in the main room of the suite while Violet finished her preparations.

"What are you doing, man?" Tony asked him in a low voice, his implications clear.

Nick met his gaze and shook his head. "Nothing. This is probably goodbye."

"You're leaving?" Tony asked, one eyebrow raised in surprise.

"Well, you and everyone else, including Violet, tell me I'm way out of my league." Nick examined his fingernails. "So what's the point of staying?"

Tony said nothing, just offered a brief nod. Thankfully, for Violet chose that moment to enter the room. Nick rushed to his feet, although that was probably a bad idea, as she was literally a knockout. He might as well have been sucker punched for the way he swayed on jelly legs.

She wore a long wine-red silky gown, which hugged her curves to the waist, then flowed about her ankles. Her hair was all pinned up and dotted with pearls, which also graced her ears and throat. Nick couldn't remember seeing anything or anyone that beautiful in all his life. Close behind that thought was the searing pain of knowing it could never be. Why had he agreed to this?

"Don't you look handsome." Violet smiled, the curve of her lips sending firebrands to his heart.

Nick cleared his throat and hitched one side of his mouth up. "You scrub up all right yourself." Yes, that's it. Downplay it. He didn't want to let her know he was completely gobsmacked, although the squeak in his voice probably gave it away.

Violet strolled over to him, her heels raising her so she didn't have to lift her chin quite so far to look at him. "Scrub up all right? I assume that's another Australian phrase."

He nodded. Gobsmacked was too, if he'd used that out loud. Totally speechless. And she smelled like heaven.

She adjusted his tie. She was close. Too close. Too, too close. He took a step backward and fell onto the sofa he'd been sitting on. "Woah."

Violet brought a hand to her mouth, giggling. "Oops. You'd better watch where you're putting those feet."

"Yeah." The one word was all he could manage as he stood and straightened his jacket. How would he ever manage dancing with her tonight? "Shall we?" He held out an elbow to escort her, sounding far more confident than he felt, especially knowing Tony trailed behind them with his protective eye on alert.

Nick relaxed into the evening as it progressed, enjoying the food, meeting other people at their table, the vibrant atmosphere around them, his conversation with Violet. In a side room, the organizers ran a silent auction to raise funds for the disadvantaged youth of Spokane. Nothing stood out to Nick, but he made a few bids since it was all for a good cause. Violet also wrote bids on a few items, not that he looked too closely. It was none of his business.

Midway through the event, the organizer stood up and gave a speech about the youth and what the funds would mean to them, giving further opportunities for people to donate. Dessert was served, and the dancing started. Nick's hands grew slick. He knew Violet loved to dance, and he didn't want to disappoint her. But he was so mesmerized, he didn't know if he could stand straight, let alone move to music.

Nick was two-thirds through his strawberry mille-feuille, which he couldn't pronounce if he tried, but delighted to eat, when the request came.

"Let's dance." Violet put a graceful hand on his forearm.

"Sure." He offered her a wobbly grin as he stood with her, conscious of Tony's eagle eye and shaking head on the side of the room.

The music was upbeat, fun songs from the fifties and sixties, with everyone trying to replicate dance moves from those eras. Nick and Violet laughed their way through several dances before Tony approached them.

"Hey, you two." He stopped them between songs.

"Yes?" Violet answered, a little out of breath.

"I'm going back to the room for a power nap before I drive you home tonight."

Wise man. It had already been a long day.

"Okay," Violet said, and Nick nodded. Although, as Tony turned away Nick was certain he gave him one of those looks that said, "behave yourself."

It was all Nick could do not to roll his eyes. He offered Tony a salute instead.

They danced a bit more until the music slowed. Couples all

around them moved into intimate dance holds. Nick and Violet stared at each other for an awkward moment. What he wouldn't give to hold her in his arms. To sway to the romantic music with her. That would be absolute heaven and absolute agony at the same time. No, he'd better not. Anyway, she'd probably push him away.

Then again, maybe she wouldn't. She'd been a bit more up-close-and-personal than usual all day. What was with that?

No, he couldn't risk it.

Nick rolled his shoulders and stretched a hand out to her as he released a breath. "Shall we get a drink?"

Was that a look of disappointment that flashed in her eyes? If it was, she shook it off. "That would be lovely. I'm thirsty after all that dancing."

She put her hand in his, and he led her to the bar. Heaven help him, her hand fit so nicely in his, he didn't want to let go. But let go, he must. He ordered them both a soda, trying to push down his ever-growing attraction. He would be returning to Australia. Nothing could come of it.

As he handed her the drink, she looked up at him. "Nick, can we talk?"

"Sure. What's up?" He gave a light shrug.

Violet dragged her bottom lip through her teeth. "I mean, talk properly. Somewhere quiet."

She headed toward the doors that led out onto a courtyard without waiting for an answer. Nick followed her, sipping his drink, wondering what she needed to talk about. Outside, away from the noise, the air was mild and bright stars washed the heavens with light above the shadowy silhouettes of mountains in the distance.

"What a beautiful night." Nick turned full circle to take it all in.

"It is, isn't it?" Violet answered, although she wasn't really looking around, but at him.

His heart skipped a beat. "What do you want to talk about?"

Violet fiddled with the straw in her drink. "I can't stop thinking about how you gave that homeless man some food today."

"So it did bother you." A twinge of disappointment rose in him. He'd never thought she was the uppity type who ignored the struggling people of the world. And she was here at this fundraiser and planning her own in the next couple months.

"Not in the way you might think," she replied, giving him some relief. "That's the sort of thing I always want to do."

Nick drew his brows together a little. "So what holds you back?"

"There is this thing in me where I always think it's wrong, or too dangerous, or a waste of time, or something like that. I'm now wondering if it's my father's voice in my head, and whether his voice might not be correct."

Nick sat down on a low wall that bordered the courtyard. "What do you mean?"

Violet sat beside him. "Ever since I was a little girl, he's always discouraged me from following my instincts. Always said my actions should be contrary to my sentiments."

Nick took a long sip of his drink. Her father sounded restrictive. And considering he had Tony watching her all the time … did he not trust her at all? Or was he just over protective? Nick needed to choose his words carefully.

"I suppose that might be sensible, sometimes. But the Lord wants us to help the disadvantaged. The Bible is very clear on this. Jesus was harsh toward those who neglect people in need. You can read the parable of the sheep and the goats in Matthew."

Violet released a deep sigh, and a tear slipped down her cheek. She ducked her chin. "I thought as much. I've been an awful selfish-looking person all my life because of my father."

Nick's heart swelled with compassion. What could he do? He

reached out and put a hand on her back. "It's okay. You know the truth now, and you don't need to live by his rules anymore." Another thought struck him. "What happened that made him so strict on you?"

"I don't know. But he definitely got worse when I was in college." Violet swallowed. "One time, I went to a party with some girls and there were guys there. They seemed nice enough and convinced me and a friend to go to the store with them to buy more supplies for the party. Instead they took us to a house, grabbed our phones off us, and locked us in a room. They were laughing and talking about how our Daddys would have to pay to get us back." Violet stopped to take a deep breath. Nick rubbed her back again.

"I was so scared. We were probably only in there for half an hour before they let us out again. It turned out they were just budding political activists who wanted to make a point, by showing us how easy it would be to kidnap us." Violet shrugged as she finished. "I just ... I had no idea. After that, Daddy hired Tony to keep me company ...and to keep me safe, I guess. Daddy and Mom have tried so hard to train me to be better."

Violet sniffed and rummaged through her purse for a tissue. "You know, they even sent me to deportment school to try and curb my behavior. Daddy wants me to be a polished, restrained businessman."

Nick pressed his lips together. "And you are a vibrant, spontaneous, generous and creative woman."

NICK SAW HER. Really saw her. No one had ever acknowledged those deep things in her heart before and it made her cry all the more. Nick's hand rubbing her back was so comforting.

"Now that you've come to know the Lord, I think he is

peeling away the layers and showing you who He intended you to be. I know that's uncomfortable right now."

Uncomfortable wasn't the word for it. She felt like a snake shedding its skin.

"Caterpillars go through an enormous struggle in their transformation into butterflies."

Violet half-laughed, half-cried at Nick's superior metaphor. She wiped at the tears and straightened.

"Thank you." Her voice wobbled.

"Tell me something," he said. "If you were free to choose, if there was nothing standing in your way, what would you do with your life?"

Violet caught her breath. That was something she'd never considered, never dared to consider, before. What would she do? Dance? She'd loved ballet as a child. Perhaps. But, oh …

"I think I'd like to help those girls rescued from trafficking. Teach them life skills. Something like that."

Nick's hand slid around her shoulder, and he squeezed. "See? There's that butterfly."

His voice sounded hoarse, and she turned her head to look at him. His eyes were glassy, and the light in them was unmistakable. Her heart fluttered at his nearness. She dropped her gaze to his lips. Right or wrong, he was the man she wanted. She leaned closer to touch her lips to his.

"No." Nick's voice was thick as he lifted a hand and placed a finger over her lips. Then he drew back from her completely, standing and rubbing his hands over his face.

The sting of rejection slammed into her. He might as well have slapped her. "What? Why? I thought—"

"You have a boyfriend, Violet."

"He's not my boyfriend."

Confusion filled Nick's face. "You said—"

"That I was seeing someone. As per my father's wishes. We've been on a few dates, nothing more. I've tried to make it work, but there is nothing there. Nothing like …" Nothing like what she felt for Nick. Not even remotely close.

Nick turned away from her and shoved his hands in his pockets. Then he swiveled back again. "But you've made it clear—everyone has made it clear—that we can't be together. And those who've assumed we are together are convinced I'm after your daddy's millions. What has changed?"

Violet rose and went to him, sliding her hands up around his neck. "Maybe I've changed. Maybe it's you I want."

"Maybe?" He searched her eyes, and she noticed his throat convulsed as he swallowed. "What about your father? Do we have a future?"

Her hands slipped back down to his chest as she averted his gaze, dropping her chin. Why did Daddy's wishes always have to come into it? Did she even have the power to defy him? "I … I don't know."

He took her hands and drew them away from him, taking a step back. "I'm not here to play games, Vi." His voice shook. "I don't want to start something that's going to end. I can't be your summer fling."

"Summer fling?" She drew her brows together. "You think this is just a temporary impulse? Do you believe I'm that shallow?"

"No … I—"

Hurt by this second rejection, she swallowed. "Do you know what? You sound just like my father."

"Seriously?" Nick's brows rose, incredulous. "Why? Because I don't act on every feeling I have?"

So he thought she was just as silly and impulsive as Daddy did. Great. "You already have, Nick. You traveled all the way here because of a feeling. And that makes you a hypocrite." With that, she collected her empty glass and stalked inside.

***

THE DRIVE back to Trinity Lakes was deathly quiet. She had no desire to speak to Nick. Thankfully, he didn't attempt any conversation either. Well, not since they got into the car. What had been a wonderful day had ended in disaster. So much for him traveling the world to find her. Violet clenched her teeth. The problem was, he was right about her father. Couldn't they just keep it a secret? See if their relationship could grow without Daddy knowing?

Who was she fooling? She wouldn't be able to hide anything with Tony always lurking around. Even without Tony, it would only take a stranger posting an innocent photo on the socials before the world knew her secret. She was surprised it hadn't erupted already. Well, except for the Trinity Lakes folk gossiping about Nick.

But the thing that grated on her most was the realization that Nick despised her "spontaneity," as he called it. He was no different from her parents who'd been reining her in for her whole life. What was so wrong with following her heart? She didn't understand. It all made her want to cry again, and she kept her face to the side window so neither Nick nor Tony would see the tears slipping down her cheeks. Well, she had asked God to take away her feelings for Nick. Perhaps His answer was to change Nick's attitude toward her. So why did it hurt so much?

When they finally pulled into the Bible College driveway and slowed to a stop, Violet stiffened. What would she say? What would Nick say? She couldn't look at him.

Rustling came from the back seat as he unbuckled and opened the door. "Um, see ya, I guess." His voice was low, awkward. A pause. A breath. Violet didn't move.

"Thanks for inviting me."

The best she could manage was a stiff nod, and then he was gone. He trudged to the front door, his shopping bags hanging from his arms, but he never looked back.

"What was that about?" Tony asked as he reversed out and headed for the country club estate.

Violet shrugged.

"You could cut the air in here with a knife. I've never been on such a long and uncomfortable drive in my life. Did he do something? Do I need to set him straight?"

"He did nothing." Which was true. She'd just wanted him to hold her and kiss her, but no, she was too emotional. "And I already set him straight."

"What happened?" Tony was clearly not going to drop it.

"All you need to know is nothing happened. And there is nothing going on between us."

Violet turned her face back to the window as tears slid down her cheeks again. Despite the hurt and anger, she wished there was something between them. He was possibly the best man she'd ever met, was ever going to meet.

Lord, help me. Show me what to do.

One thing she was sure of. She had to break it off with Alistair. As soon as she was home and away from Tony, she pulled her phone out and hit the call icon on Alistair's number. Violet hoped he was still awake at this time of the night—or morning.

CHAPTER ELEVEN

Well, Nick had really messed that up, hadn't he? He checked his phone for the time. Three a.m., and he hadn't slept a wink. His stomach still churned. He hadn't meant to upset Violet. Not in a million years.

If only she knew how hard it was for him to resist taking her in his arms and kissing the life out of her. But for him, it was all or nothing. If he kissed her, he'd lose his heart to her forever. And with all the uncertainty surrounding her father's wishes, he couldn't risk it.

But now she thought him a hypocrite. The accusation stung. Nick checked his phone again. Three forty-five. This was useless. He got up and paced the room before heading to the kitchen for a glass of water. Grabbing his phone and earbuds from his room, he sat in a recliner in the living room and put worship music on, hoping it would calm him.

What was he going to do? Although he'd tried to apologize several times before they even got into the car, she refused to respond. He'd never experienced the silent treatment before. None of his sisters ever did it, and neither did his parents—not even to each other. How was he supposed to sort out a problem if he couldn't even talk it out? Ugh.

But she had said she was interested in him. Wanted him. Nick's stomach convulsed again. Hearing those words nearly undid him. What he wouldn't give for a chance to sort this out. That moment had been everything he hoped for and everything he dreaded all at once. And now what? So close to his dream and yet so impossibly far. Should he give up and go home?

Images of deep shadowy chasms scrolled through his mind. He stood on the cliff above, balanced precariously on the edge. There was Violet, Princess Jasmine, across the other side, her back to him. There was no way down, no way across. Another figure walked toward her and tugged at her arm, dragging her away. Then she looked over her shoulder at him.

"Nick," she called, her voice desperate. "Nick? Nick…?"

Nick started awake to see Lexi standing over the recliner.

"What are you doing, sleeping out here?"

"Oh." He rubbed his face and pulled the earbuds from his ears. He must have finally drifted off. "Rough night."

She tilted her head sideways. "How was the gala?"

Fantastic? Terrible? Magic? Worst night of his life? "Unexpected." Nick didn't want to talk about it. He'd already been going over and over it all night. "What time is it?"

"Just gone seven. You okay?"

"Yep." Nick pushed himself out of the recliner. "Think I need a shower." Less than three hours' sleep and a fog of confusion left him feeling heavy. A hot shower might help. And then back to bed. Forget church. Not today. Everything was falling apart, and he didn't think he could face smiling people or joyful worship. Nope. He just needed more sleep so he could think straight again. He brushed past Lexi and headed for the bathroom. He'd apologize for his rudeness later.

———

AT ELEVEN, a loud thumping on the front door and incessant pressing of the doorbell dragged him from sleep again. Nick pulled the covers over his head, trying to ignore it, make it go away. Didn't whoever it was know the Franklins were all at church at this time on a Sunday? He groaned. Precious. He needed sleep. *Please, let me sleep.*

The thumping came again, followed by a loud voice. "Nick Gordon. I know you're in there."

What? Who?

Nick sat up and rubbed his eyes, then shook his head, trying to remove the wet socks that seemed to have lodged in there. Whose voice was that? He didn't recognize it. And it sounded like a voice that wouldn't accept no for an answer. He groaned again and forced himself upward. Stumbling to the front door, he realized he probably looked a fright. Great.

He pulled open the door and squinted into the sunlight to see a man with salt and pepper hair, sporting a blazer and open-collared shirt despite the warmth of the morning.

"Nick Gordon?" The man's voice was stern. And Nick's stomach tightened at something familiar in his face.

"Yeah."

"A word, if you don't mind."

"May I know who I'm talking to?" Nick asked, wary.

"Morgan Reynolds."

Nick gulped, his suspicions confirmed. Violet's father. Here, on his doorstep. This could only mean trouble. But he drew the door wide open to welcome him in. No sense in starting off on the wrong foot more than he already had.

"Pleased to meet you." Nick's voice squeaked. "Sorry. I was asleep." Point one against him. For a tycoon, Nick no doubt looked lazy. Great first impression.

"Can I get you a coffee?" *That's right Nick, be hospitable.*

"I'm not here for a social call, Mr. Gordon."

Okaaaay. Nick waved him toward the living room, apprehension shifting his heart rate into overdrive. And he'd thought being around Violet was nerve-racking enough.

But Mr. Reynolds did not sit. Instead, he rounded on Nick, one finger pointed straight into his chest. "You have some nerve if you think you have any chance with my girl."

Woah. This man barely contained his impatience. Nick stood still. He didn't want to appear intimidated, even if his insides were shaking like jelly. "I am well aware I have no chance." That's right. Keep his voice steady.

That seemed to settle him a little. Mr. Reynolds shoved his hands in his pockets. "Then what do you think you are trying to achieve by insinuating yourself into her life?"

"Insinuating?" Nick figured the less he said, the safer he was at this stage. If he let his tongue loose, he'd probably incriminate himself. Besides, Nick was unsure what or how much Violet's dad knew.

"I've just learned you're the one who duped her in Australia last year. Are you here to deceive her again? Do you think she's just an easy mark?"

Nick cleared his throat. "Sir, I thought we, that is Vi—Miss Reynolds and I already cleared up that misunderstanding. I am not and have never been an employee of TESView. I was filling in for the day and knew nothing of Vi—Miss Reynolds's purpose in being there. She has already confirmed this information with the company."

Mr. Reynolds stopped and stared at him. Oh. Had Violet not told him the truth? Reynolds withdrew his cell phone and tapped a message. Then he looked back at Nick, frown still in place.

"Regardless. Now you're here in America training her to skydive. I suppose you put that idea in her head.

"No, sir. I—"

"And then there's this." Mr. Reynolds tapped on his screen again and turned it to face Nick.

Images of him dancing in the store in Spokane with Violet. On social media. Damning photos if ever he saw them. Particularly one photo, where it was clear how Nick felt about her from the look on his face. And Violet's eyes weren't devoid of emotion either. How come he'd not seen that before?

"We were just messing around." Why did his voice have to sound so high-pitched? He tried for a chuckle, but it sounded more like a whimper in his ears. How he wished even one member of the Franklin family was home right now.

"So what are you after? Money? I can give you money. Whatever you want. You just need to walk away."

Seriously? Nick pushed down the indignation that rose like hot lava in a volcano. He could not afford to erupt. Not now. Not like this. If only he'd had more sleep. If only he could think straight. But his brain was only going in one direction.

"I'm not interested in your money, *sir*." He grated out the word. "And I think you should let your daughter make her own decisions."

"Excuse me?" Mr. Reynolds's face changed color and his brow lowered even further.

Precious. Did he have a death wish? Possibly. The problem was, he wasn't done. "Violet has excellent instincts. She has amazing, creative ideas. You should listen to her and trust her more than you do."

"You presume to tell me how to parent my own child?" Mr. Reynolds wasn't yelling, but, oh, it felt like it. "She is spoken for. Do you hear me? Stay away from her." His finger was back in Nick's face.

Too angry to be reasonable now, Nick kept his face like flint. "I will make no such promise."

"And you will deal with the consequences if you ignore me." Mr. Reynolds stalked to the door. Good. He was leaving. Without another word, he stormed to his flashy sports car and took off in a spray of gravel.

Nick sucked in a deep breath. Did Violet's father just threaten him? Well, it didn't matter. He was going to book tickets back to Australia as soon as possible.

———

IT WAS hard to concentrate on Pastor Wilder's message with a thousand questions coursing through Violet's mind, interspersed with angry, hurt-filled thoughts. No matter how she tried, she only managed to shut them down for a few minutes at a time. Then the same barrage started over again. She just couldn't make sense of it. Just when she realized Nick was the one she wanted, he decided he didn't want her.

Well, at least she'd gotten one thing sorted out. Alistair had sounded sleepy when he answered her call yet had the grace to listen to her tearful apology. Guilt niggled in the pit of Violet's stomach. The tears hadn't been for Alistair, but for the hurt resulting from her conversation with Nick. She didn't tell Alistair about her feelings for Nick, rather telling only half the truth —that she didn't have the right feelings for Alistair. Couldn't see their relationship developing into anything meaningful. Didn't think they had a future together.

Alistair was silent for a while, a long while.

"Alistair? Are you going to say anything?"

He cleared his throat. "I guess I'll cancel my flight for tomorrow."

That was it? No pleading with her to reconsider? No angry outburst? Not even a single question? "I guess so."

And that was it. A brief goodbye, and he was gone. Violet didn't know if he was relieved, upset, angry, hurt, anything. She hoped he hadn't taken it badly. Hoped he hadn't felt something more for her. Hoped he hadn't formed a strong attachment to her. It wasn't like they'd got really close, even though he'd moved to kiss her that one time.

The congregation stood around her. Wow. She'd been so lost in her thoughts, she hadn't even heard Pastor Wilder finish his sermon. More guilt to add to the pile. She made a lousy Christian. She forced herself to pay attention to the rest of the service, the little that remained.

Tony filed out of the pew ahead of her and they made their way to the doors.

"How's the fundraiser coming along, Violet?"

Violet turned to see Liam Darcy, flanked by his wife, Elissa.

"Hello, Liam. Elissa. It's coming together nicely. It should be a fantastic event. Will you come along on the day?"

"We wouldn't miss it." Elissa slipped an arm around her husband's waist with a grin. "Is there anything I can do to help?"

"Thanks. We've got an event coordinator managing everything now. But I can give them your name, if you like?"

"Yes, do that," she replied. "In fact, I can probably muster up a few volunteers from church, if that would help."

"That would be amazing. Thank you."

"I hear you've managed to get Mitchell Reilly up in the sky." Liam's lips twitched in amusement.

"Yes, I have." Violet grinned in response.

"That will be fun." Liam slipped his hand into Elissa's. "We'll see you around."

Violet sighed, watching them walk away. Such a lovely couple. If only she could have a relationship like that.

When Tony pulled into the driveway minutes later, a bright yellow sports car sat in front of the house. That could only mean one thing. Daddy was here. It had been an age since he came to visit her.

Violet jumped out of the car as soon as it stopped and raced into the house.

"Daddy," she called.

There he was, waiting in the living room. Violet ran into his arms. "It's so good to see you."

It was comforting to be held right now, even for a moment, but her father soon pushed her back to arm's length. "And you, sweet pea." He brushed her hair away from her face. "We'll catch up soon. Right now, I'd like you to go pack a suitcase. I'm sending you to France for an assignment."

"You said I was having a break from travel until the end of summer."

"I know. But this opportunity has come up, and we don't want to miss it."

"What about my fundraiser?" And the skydiving. And her new friends. And Nick.

"It's only for a week or two. You'll be back before you know it. Now, go do as I ask."

Violet searched his eyes for a moment. There was something unflinching in them. Something he wasn't telling her. "What's wrong, Daddy?"

"Later, Vi. Go pack."

There was no use arguing. Daddy would always have his way. She hurried to her room, changed into comfortable clothes for traveling, and tossed items into her suitcase. Violet had packed so many times in the last couple of years, she packed almost by instinct. What was so urgent about this trip? And why had Daddy needed to come all the way here to collect her? Something was off. Did it have to do with her breaking things off with Alistair? Would Alistair have told Daddy so quickly? Perhaps. They did work fairly closely together on the proposed merger.

Violet tucked her travel journal in the outer pocket of her suitcase, then eyed last year's journal still sitting on her bedside. Why not? She grabbed it and added it to her bag. She'd lost count of how many times she'd reread about that day with Nick. The more she read it, the more she realized they had a genuine connection from the first moment.

Raised voices trickled up the stairs. Were Daddy and Tony

arguing? That was new. What was going on? Then the door slammed. That couldn't be good. Violet tossed some bathroom items into a toiletry bag and put it in her suitcase. She straightened and eyed the room, making sure she had everything she needed. Oh, her passport. That was important. Retrieving it from her bedside table drawer, she collected her bags and headed back downstairs.

"Where's Tony?"

"He's not coming." Daddy wasn't giving much away.

"What about Amelia?"

"She'll meet us in Seattle tomorrow morning. Are you ready? Let's go."

So curt. So blunt. Not that it was a surprise. He was a high-powered businessman. Blunt was how he got the job done. But he wasn't usually so abrupt with Violet.

"I haven't eaten."

"We'll get some lunch on the way."

It wasn't until they were twenty minutes down the road that Daddy finally opened up. "I cannot believe you got yourself tied up with that fraud again."

"Fraud? Who …?" Oh, the truth clicked into place.

"Nick Gordon. Although he seems to think you know all about him."

Violet swallowed. "You spoke to Nick?"

Daddy's hands twisted on the steering wheel. "Yes."

"And did he tell you he's no fraud?" Violet focused on her breathing. If she started fuming at him now, he would shut the conversation down.

"The question is, why didn't *you* tell me?"

There it was again. Zero trust. "It was easy enough to verify, which I'm sure you have done already. I figured you'd tell me to stay away from him, even if he was innocent."

"Yes, and that is exactly what I am doing."

"Why?" That was the only word that entered her mind.

"Maybe he wasn't out to trick you in Australia, but he most certainly is after something now."

Daddy's previous words hit her again. He'd been to see Nick. Oh no, no, no. What had he said? And what had Nick said? She had no idea. All she could do was play ignorant.

"What makes you so sure?"

Daddy took his phone from the console and handed it to her. "Have a look at the photos I happened upon yesterday."

Violet drew another deep breath. What could he be referring to? She opened his phone and found the photos. In the store, dancing and messing about. Oh, there was even a brief video clip. Violet bit down on her lip to hide the smile that wanted to spread. If it were anyone else, she would say "cute couple." Couple. Oh. That's what Daddy saw. A couple. Yes, affection was definitely evident in those pictures.

With a sigh, she replaced the phone. "We're just friends, Daddy."

"You need to stay away from him."

And suddenly it all became clear. Daddy was taking her away from Nick. Forcing her away. Had he used the same heavy-handedness on Nick? Tears welled in her eyes.

"Why do you never trust me?"

Violet glanced sideways at her father as tears trickled down her cheeks. His lips pressed into a grim line. "Because you consistently show me I can't."

"What else have I done wrong?" Violet felt like a small child again. She fished around in her purse for a tissue. When would Daddy ever be happy with her?

"Alistair called me this morning."

He didn't need to explain further.

"I don't love him, Daddy."

"So you love Nick Gordon?"

"I never said that. We are friends." But, yes, maybe she did. A little. Maybe even a lot.

"I will not let you throw your future away on some no-hoper Australian."

"You know nothing about him."

"And you do?"

"He's an experienced skydive instructor, an electrician, and a talented musician." Violet bit her lip. Her words made it obvious she'd spent time with him.

"Another thing you neglected to tell me." A scornful laugh left his mouth. "He's your skydiving instructor."

"I'm sorry." Violet closed her eyes and faced away from him, tears still rolling down her cheeks.

"And you can't see that he's manipulating you to get what he wants? He's got you right where he wants you. I can't believe you'd hide all this from me."

There was no way she could make him understand. No way he'd believe that Nick's being at Freefall Adventures was a coincidence. And no way he'd accept that she was drawn to his shared faith.

CHAPTER TWELVE

Nick phoned Mud. Sure, it was just after two in the morning in the Northern Territory, but Nick needed to hear a friendly voice. He hadn't realized how much he appreciated his friend's presence with him here until he left.

"Dude. So late." Mud groaned.

"Tell me you were asleep and I'll hang up."

"You know me too well. I was just about to get some shuteye now. What's up?"

"Everything." Nick paced his room.

Silence for a moment. "Bro. C'mon. You don't sound good. What happened?"

If Mud had been on the verge of sleep, he now sounded completely alert.

It was hard for Nick to make himself say the words. To admit failure. "We were so close. Then I said something stupid, and now she's not even talking to me."

"How close are we talking?"

"Close enough." Nick couldn't articulate the way her nearness had shaken him.

Another pause. "Does this have something to do with that dumb pact you made with yourself?"

Nick rubbed his face. Here it came. "Maybe."

"You're such an idiot, dude. What's wrong with a bit of kissing?"

Nick had been over this with Mud before and he wasn't about to go there again. "I didn't ring you for a lecture."

"What did you ring me for, then?"

Sometimes, Mud could be the most insensitive ... "Never mind." Nick prepared to hit the end call button.

"Wait. Sorry, bro. Does Vi know about your vow of celibacy or whatever it is?"

"No."

"You probably should tell her."

"Except she won't talk to me. And to make it worse, her father came and told me to back off this morning."

"What? Dude. He came over?"

"Yes, he literally flew from Seattle, then drove here to interrogate me and warn me off. What am I going to do?" Nick rubbed his hand down his face. "I should just come home, yeah? I mean, it's not worth this amount of trouble, is it? Morgan Reynolds holds a lot of power. Power I have zero chance of fighting."

"If Violet's in, who cares?"

Nick closed his eyes. "I don't think she'll defy her father. She loves him. Idolizes him." Sure, she'd talked about other dreams last night, but would she ever step out and try to follow them? He doubted she'd go against her father's wishes.

"I'm sorry, bro. I hoped this would work out for you." Mud yawned.

"Me too. I'll let you get some sleep. Thanks, mate."

"Yep. See ya when you get home."

Then Mud was gone. So Mud thought he should quit and go back to Australia, too. Well, that was that.

An hour later, Peter Franklin handed Nick a soda before sitting across the dining table from him with a cup of coffee. "What's that you're doing?"

Nick had his laptop open in front of him, scrolling through the next flights available to get him back home to Darwin. "Booking airfares." He leaned back and opened the can, taking a sip.

"You're going home?"

"I've stuffed up right royally. I should never have come. It was lunacy. Like you said, a waste of time." Even acknowledging his failure felt like another knife in the gut.

"Hold on a minute." Peter twisted his mug on the table.

"What?"

"Maybe I spoke in haste."

A scornful laugh escaped. "No. No, you didn't. It's never going to happen." Nick couldn't bring himself to admit what Morgan Reynolds had said this morning.

Silence for a moment. "There's this little video that's gaining traction on the socials." Peter pulled his phone out of his pocket. "Rhonda Turner showed this to me."

"Isn't she one of the people who's been gossiping about me?"

"Well, yes, but we don't pay heed to gossip." He turned his phone around to show Nick the clip of him and Violet dancing in the store. "It seems like you two have gotten closer than I ever thought you would."

Great. Now he had to tell him. "Her father has told me in no uncertain terms that I have no chance."

"Really? That's harsh." Peter winced and shifted in his seat. "However, if the Lord has made a way thus far, surely He can finish the job."

"That's just it. I'm not sure He's in it." Nick took another drink. It was all too confusing.

Peter stared at him for a while. "Can I ask, since when did the Bible say, 'Seek ye first the kingdom of Violet Reynolds?'"

What? Woah. Where did that come from? Nick opened his mouth to object, but his mind was spinning with the depth in Peter's words.

"If the Lord brought you here, I can assure you it wasn't only for a girl. He has other purposes for you here in Trinity Lakes. Have you asked Him about that? Have you tried to make other connections? Be involved in the community or church life—other than attending a Bible study during the week?"

Yikes. Nick felt like those words stripped him naked. Exposed. He had no answer. Well, no defense. Nick hadn't considered any of that. He'd only focused on Violet, and even though he'd prayed about her often, he hadn't sought the Lord's will, assuming he already knew it. How pious that sounded.

Nick swallowed. "I—I don't …"

"May I suggest you hold off booking those tickets? Have a think about it. Have a think about your employer at the airfield. You made commitments when you came here. Are they negated because things aren't going your way? Don't rush this decision. Spend some time in prayer."

Nick immediately shut the laptop. "Yeah, you're right. I'll do that." It was unlike him to make an emotional decision—the very thing he'd accused Violet of last night. Talk about not seeing the log in his own eye. He had some serious self-reflection to do.

Trouble was, he still felt awful after last night's argument, his lack of sleep, and Morgan Reynold's accusations. The first order would be to get some rest so he could think straight. He thanked Peter and headed to his room.

Later in the afternoon, Nick grabbed his earbuds and went out to the ride-on mower. Cutting the lawns might be cathartic and would give him a chance to think and pray, with the soothing melodies of worship in the background.

Pete had been right. Nick had single-mindedly pursued Violet while professing to keep his distance most of the time. He could have said no to any of the opportunities he'd had to be near her. To the nightclub and cafe, the picnic, the gala dinner. But he'd excused himself because he hadn't created the opportunities. Told himself it was okay because the invitations dropped into his lap. All along, his conscience told him to stay away because she had a boyfriend. Or maybe that was the Lord. Nick was precisely the hypocrite Violet had called him.

Nick put the brake on the mower and closed his eyes, leaning forward on the steering wheel. "Sorry Lord. I haven't been listening to you. I've been listening to the desires of my heart and running after the dream I thought you gave me without seeking you on how and when." He continued to pray for some time, recommitting himself to the Lord and praying that God would comfort and heal Violet from any hurt he'd caused. Finally, he put the future of his relationship with Violet Reynolds into the Lord's hands.

As he released the brake and continued mowing, he sensed a release within. He still felt somewhat miserable, and there was still a long road ahead, but no matter what it contained, the Lord was with him.

DADDY WAS STILL GIVING her the silent treatment. The entire flight back to Seattle, he'd not spoken a word to her, though she'd tried to reignite the argument several times. Much like the drive back from Spokane with Nick. Is that where she'd learned that behavior from—Daddy? Violet tracked back through her memory. Yes, there were many times he'd shut down communication when he was angry, making her feel insignificant. Was that how Nick felt now? A twinge of guilt niggled at her.

The only information she'd dragged out of Daddy was that Tony no longer worked for the company and, therefore, was no longer her security chaperone. Her father planned to replace

Tony with someone new for this trip to France. Violet couldn't even get her father to talk about why Tony was suddenly gone after so many years. She shed several more tears over that. Tony had been like a second father. And he was the person who'd led her to faith. She'd miss him terribly. What would the new guy be like?

Now Daddy had gone off for some business meeting, leaving her to spend the afternoon and evening with Mom before flying out in the morning. Violet snuggled into the sofa with her mother as they watched an emotional movie and nibbled on popcorn. The problem was that the emotional scenes made her cry more than usual. She was too vulnerable right now.

"What's going on, honey?" Mom paused the film and turned to face her. "I know your father is being tough on you, but is that all that's upsetting you?"

"How much do you know?" Violet pulled out a tissue and wiped her eyes.

"I know he's not happy with the company you've been keeping."

"Did he tell you Tony resigned or something?"

"Oh. No, I hadn't heard that part. I'm sorry, darling. That must hurt."

Violet picked up a cushion and hugged it to her chest, plucking at the edge tassels. "I don't understand why he's so insistent on Alistair. I understand there is a business merger to take into consideration, but I don't comprehend why that can't happen if I'm not married to Alistair. Why can't I choose my life partner myself? Why don't you guys trust me?"

Mom drew in a deep breath and twisted her wedding rings around her finger. "It's not that we don't trust you."

"That's what it feels like. 'Whatever is in your head, do the opposite.' That's what Daddy always says." And his voice in her head often stopped her from doing good things, maybe even important things.

Mom swallowed and cleared her throat. "I think perhaps we made a mistake. Early on." She shifted in her seat, seeming uncomfortable with the confession. "When you were a little girl, you were so friendly and bubbly. You'd talk to any and everyone. If we were at a funeral, you would cuddle any person who was crying, even if they were a complete stranger."

"What's wrong with wanting to comfort the bereaved?"

"We didn't know who might take advantage of our compassionate and generous little girl. So, I guess we squashed that in you by telling you to stop every time you wanted to help someone or care for someone or befriend a homeless drunk, or whatever. Especially if there was the possibility of kidnap and ransom because of your daddy's wealth. Looking back, I think we did more harm than good."

The incident at college wouldn't have helped.

"Your father thought self-discipline was the answer. After all, discipline and organization was how he built his empire. So we enrolled you in dance lessons, finishing school, anything that had strict disciplinary teaching. I think we've tried to push a round and beautiful peg into a sharp-edged square hole, and I am increasingly sorry for that."

Violet stared at her mother. Why had she never heard all this before? Suddenly, everything made sense. They had been trying to make her into something she was not just as Nick had said. Now she was learning who she was in Jesus, He was showing her the truth of her identity. It was like scales fell from her eyes, although tears still streamed down her cheeks.

"Thank you, Mom. You cannot imagine what it means to me to hear you explain that. I wish I'd known sooner, but now it's so clear."

Mom scooted closer and enfolded her in a long and tight embrace. "I'm sorry, honey. So sorry."

When they finally pulled away from each other, Mom smiled

gently. "So tell me about this young man that has your father ruffled."

"He's overreacting, Mom." Violet examined her fingernails. "Nick and I are just friends." Were friends. Could be friends. Could be more than friends if circumstances were different.

"But you like him, don't you?" Mom ducked her head to peer into Violet's lowered eyes.

It was no use pretending to her mother. She'd see straight through Violet anyway. "Yes, I do. But it's okay. He knows there can't be anything between us."

After talking some more, and sorting through some emotions Mom's words had raised, Violet went to her bedroom —one her parents always kept for her—to spend more time thinking and praying.

It was strange. Perhaps this impulsive side of her nature wasn't a bad thing after all. And yet, she still felt guilty each time she acted spontaneously. Daddy didn't appreciate it. Mom, well, Mom kind of accepted it. But Nick, despite encouraging her, had let slip that he thought impulsivity was bad.

Despite his claims of having come to America for her, despite the compliments he'd thrown her way, maybe he didn't mean any of it. Maybe Daddy was right. Maybe Nick had been manipulating her all along. It was all too confusing.

Violet picked up a manila folder her father had given her, trying to push all her jumbled thoughts aside. The folder outlined her itinerary in France. She was to join a luxury ten-day tour of Southern France and evaluate their services and experiences. Her stomach fluttered a little. What if she made the same mistake she'd made in Australia?

Violet shook her head. No, because there would be no Nick Gordon. At least, she hoped there wouldn't be. What if another handsome man came her way and flattered her into thinking he was someone special? Was she that susceptible? No. Again. A gorgeous smile had never swayed her before. Not since Lyall.

Lyall. She hadn't thought about him in months. Lyall, whom she'd practically grown up with and assumed she'd end up marrying. She'd been besotted with him for years, yet she now realized she'd still never felt quite like she felt with Nick.

Violet groaned and threw herself back onto her bed. Why was life and love so hard? Just when she found someone she thought she might truly love, he turned out to be a fake. She'd thought Nick cared, but now she realized her personality repulsed him. She groaned again. She needed to stop thinking about him.

Oh. Violet sat up with a start as a thought struck her. She was going to France. How was she going to continue her skydiving training? This could ruin the fundraising event. She hadn't completed enough jumps to do her assessment dive, and being away for almost two weeks meant missing multiple opportunities to practice.

She picked up her phone and sent a message to Amelia to contact Freefall Adventures. Hopefully Frank Martinez would know how to help her.

CHAPTER THIRTEEN

On Monday morning, Nick had a shift at the airfield. Hopefully Violet had booked in for some practice jumps, as he really needed to apologize to her. Even if they had no future, he didn't want bad blood between them.

Upon entering the hangar, he checked the bookings diary carefully, leafing through pages to find her name. Nothing. Not today. Not tomorrow. Nothing for the entire week. His brows furrowed together as he turned to Frank.

"I see Violet hasn't booked in at all this week. Is something wrong?" He hoped she hadn't quit the whole thing because of him. That would be a huge shame. She had a large event riding on this, although the fundraiser could go ahead without her participating in the formation dive.

"Not exactly," Frank said. "She's gone to France for a work trip."

"What?" When did that happen? It must have been sudden. And how did Frank know? Of course, Violet wasn't speaking to Nick, so she hadn't shared it with him.

"Her assistant called an hour ago. I'm going to find her a contact in France so she can complete some more practice dives while she's away."

"Oh. Right." Nick was partly relieved. She hadn't quit. But overseas? How was he meant to make things up to her now? "Do you know how long she is away?"

"Two weeks, I think."

Man, she was cutting it close. And she still needed to complete her assessment dive. Why would she go on a business trip now? Wasn't she supposed to be having a summer-long break from travel? Hadn't her father …?

Her father.

Of course.

Morgan Reynolds was determined to keep them apart. Frustration churned in Nick as he prepared his first client for a tandem jump. What did Mr. Reynolds have against him anyway? Other than Nick not being an up-and-coming tycoon?

As he dropped out of the plane with his client, he breathed out. He needed to trust the Lord, just like this young teenager trusted Nick to get him safely to the ground. Just like Nick trusted in the canopy to open and stop them from plunging to their deaths. The Lord would lead him safely and securely in the purposes He had for Nick.

At the end of the shift, Nick folded himself into the tiny hatchback and pulled out his phone. It was seven-thirty a.m. Tuesday for his parents. Hopefully, he could catch them before their day got underway.

"Hi, Mum." He waved through the screen. It was so good to see her face. Missing his family was the hardest part of this gig.

"Nicky!" She almost squealed. She swiveled her head to announce to anyone else in the house that he was on the phone.

Next thing, they were all crowding around her. Two of his sisters were eating breakfast, toast in hand, and his dad held a steaming mug. But they all waved excitedly at him and greeted him with blown kisses and virtual hugs. One by one, they handed the phone around, and one by one they had a brief chat with him before they had to head off to work or jump in the shower or whatever was on their agenda for the day.

Soon it was just Mum again. She wouldn't be in a hurry to go anywhere.

"They're all looking great." Nick wished he'd been able to physically hug them all.

"Yes, there's a bit of excitement at the moment."

"Why's that?"

"Cathy and Isaac have set a date for their wedding."

Cathy was the oldest of his younger sisters. A lump formed in his throat. Wedding preparations were beginning, and he wouldn't be there for them. Perhaps he would be home in time for the wedding. The way things were going …

"That's awesome. I'm happy for them." He was, but it didn't quite carry through to his voice.

"On the downside, Uncle Will is in hospital. He went into a diabetic coma. He'll be okay, but it was touch and go for a bit. Keep him in your prayers, will you?"

Another hit. It was hard to hear Mum's news and know he couldn't be there. "Of course I will. Are you okay, Mum?"

"I'm all right. God is good. But I won't say I wasn't scared for a day or two."

"Oh, Mum. I wish I was there for you." Nick felt a vise around his heart.

"I know, love." She drew a deep breath. "How about you? What's happening over there in Trinity Lakes?"

"Not much, to be honest." Nick updated her on what had happened with Violet since they last spoke.

When he finished, she was quiet for a while. "Well, I have to say I agree with Pete Franklin. You need to pray more about this. I don't sense you should come home right now, despite how much we miss you and would love to have you here."

Nick swallowed. For a mother to tell her son not to come

home was significant. And she well knew how homesick he could get.

"I know it's hard, bub, but you love her, right?"

Nick lifted his gaze to meet her eyes. "How can you—?"

"It's all over your face when you talk about her." Mum giggled. "You should reach out to her. Clear the air."

"What about her father?"

"An apology won't hurt anyone," Mum said. "I'm looking forward to meeting this girl. She sounds pretty special."

Nick felt warmth flood to his cheeks. "She is, Mum. She is."

After he ended the call, Nick sat in the car for a few minutes, pondering. He'd never allowed himself to admit it before, but yes, he loved Violet. Loved her in a way he never thought possible. And now he had to let it go. Stop trying. Stop striving. Just trust.

Yikes, but the afternoon sun was hot. He needed to get the engine and air-conditioning going. Forty-five minutes later, he pulled into the Trinity Life Church parking lot. Time to follow through on another part of Pete's advice.

"Pastor Ladan?" Nick knocked gently on the open office door.

The man looked up from his desk.

"Could I have a word?" Did the pastor recognize him? "I'm Nick Gordon. I'm staying with the Franklins at the Bible College."

"Good to see you, Nick." Pastor Ladan stood from his chair and held out a hand, which Nick shook. "What's on your mind?"

He motioned for Nick to take a seat and he did so. "I know I haven't been here long, and I'm not sure how long I'll be around, but I'd like to be involved. Volunteer in some capacity."

"That's great, Nick." Pastor Ladan seemed happy. "We can use all the help we can get. Tell me about yourself."

"Okay." Nick launched into a list of his skills and expertise.

"I suspect we can't use your skydiving abilities here. We're more about sending people heavenward than hurling them to the ground."

"Yeah, right." Nick laughed. Why had he even mentioned skydiving? Probably nerves, although he couldn't figure out why.

"And I'm probably not going to put you on the stage with the worship team, given you are unsure about your commitment here."

"Of course." And why would he? Nick was still relatively unknown.

"However, we have an electrical circuit that keeps tripping, and some flickering lights. I'd love it if you can have a look. And there are a few other odd jobs and repairs if you think you can manage them."

Nick grinned. Perhaps he could be useful after all. "Sure, I can do that. You'd have to get someone else to sign off if there's something major wrong with the electrical wiring, as I'm not registered here, but I can certainly fix anything minor."

"And the handyman stuff?"

"Yeah, that too."

"Great."

"When would you like me to come?"

"When are you free?"

Nick left the church with a smile on his face. It felt good to be giving back. Sure, he'd been doing maintenance at the college, but this was different. This wasn't in exchange for accommodation or food or anything. He sighed. Back at home, he was always involved in the church activities, leading the worship, helping out with their electrics. He'd forgotten the sense of belonging it gave him. Thank God for Pete Franklin and his wise advice.

Nick tucked himself into the little hatchback and pulled out his phone. Right or wrong, he needed to tell Violet he was sorry.

———

VVIOLET'S PHONE pinged with several message notifications. So did Amelia's and Drew's, the new guy. He seemed a few years younger than Tony, but still much older than Violet. And much sterner than Tony. She hadn't seen him smile once.

They'd just arrived in Paris for a layover before flying to Nice in a couple of hours. Here in Paris it was breakfast time, even as her body screamed it was the middle of the night. When they finally sat down in the business class lounge, she picked up her phone and looked at the screen. Yes, just after midnight in Washington. Jet lag was going to be a killer.

Messages. Messages. Messages.

From Mom and Daddy checking in on her. From Bree with a "what the heck" tirade about her sudden disappearance from Trinity Lakes. From Tony with a simple "I'm sorry."

And one from Nick.

She put the phone down, unwilling to read whatever he had to say, even though her heart skipped a beat just seeing his name.

"Any news?" she asked Amelia.

"The event organizers have some questions about the fundraiser."

"That can wait until we're settled in Nice." She was too tired to think right now.

"Freefall Adventures have sent through a contact link for you."

"Great." That could also wait until she'd caught up on some sleep. She plugged her phone charger into an available socket and leaned back in the velour seat with her eyes closed.

"Aren't you going to read it?" Amelia asked.

"Read what?" Violet opened her eyes and pointedly looked at Drew, who was busy checking his own phone. Hopefully Amelia got the message, because Daddy would undoubtedly hear about any mention of Nick.

Amelia nodded slightly. "The message from *Ned*, the tour guide from *Flanders*, Belgium. I saw his name pop up on your screen before. He probably wants to *apologize* for ... getting the booking wrong?"

Good girl. Although she should probably stop meddling.

"He got it wrong all right." And he was someone else who could wait. Maybe wait until she went home. "Right now, I want a power nap. Is that okay, my super-efficient PA? No more business." Violet tried to follow up with a smile, but it probably came out as a grimace given the twinge of guilt that went with it. Amelia didn't deserve to be the recipient of her irritation.

It wasn't until they'd settled into their five-star hotel and caught a couple of hours of proper sleep that Violet's curiosity grew enough to read the message from Nick. And now there were two more, all silly GIFs that said sorry in different ways— a puppy-dog with big sorry eyes, a man declaring he was an idiot, a person pulling a paper bag over their head in shame.

Violet smiled and bit her lip. She didn't want to be won over that easily. What he'd said still hurt. She paused with her fingers over the keypad. What should she reply? She didn't want to make it worse by being awful, but she didn't want to pretend it was all okay. In the end, she shut off her phone and went to find Amelia. They needed to keep themselves awake until French bedtime now, so they could be ready for the tour tomorrow.

Within half an hour, the three of them sat at an outdoor cafe along one of the main streets in Nice, with coffees and French pastries.

"What we need to do is go over this itinerary and work out when I can slip away to do some practice dives," Violet told Amelia.

Amelia swallowed a sip of her macchiato. "I've already had a good look for you. You have a couple of free mornings, one just out of Marseille, and one near Montpellier. Will that be enough?"

"Hold on, ladies." A frown creased Drew's brow. "What's this about?"

Violet let out an impatient huff. "I've been training for a skydiving license, and I need to finish my practice jumps, so I can be ready for my fundraiser."

"Mr. Reynolds did not mention this." Drew sounded suspicious.

"I'm not exactly surprised," Violet said. "He threw me on a plane with little warning. I doubt he thought about it. But it is important, and I will complete those dives, whether you accompany me or not." She stared him straight in the eye, giving him no doubt about her determination.

Drew raised two hands in mock surrender. "Very well. Am I expected to jump out of the plane with you?"

Violet giggled then, her tension easing. "Only if you want to. Amelia is happy to keep her feet on the ground, aren't you, Amelia?"

Amelia laughed. "It's bad enough I have to get on jumbo jets with you, let alone fly up in a tiny plane and be tossed out midflight." She nibbled a pastry. "I'll watch from the safety of the tarmac, thank you."

Later that night, after they'd locked the door of their hotel suite and Drew had finally left them alone, Amelia turned to Violet.

"Have you contacted Nick yet?"

Violet busied herself with preparing for bed. "No."

"Are you going to?"

Violet lifted one shoulder. She saw Amelia shake her head from the corner of her eye.

"The longer you leave it, the harder it gets."

"Thank you, wise one." Violet rolled her eyes. "I will. When I'm ready."

However, two days of the tour passed and she still hadn't figured out what to say to Nick Gordon, despite his numerous and frequent messages. More GIFs. More simple text messages.

Sorry.

Please talk to me.

Thankfully, he'd stopped sending them. Thankfully? Not true. She was checking and rechecking her phone, to the extent she annoyed herself.

Maybe he'd given up. Disappointment churned, realizing she didn't want him to give up, yet, she didn't feel ready to contact him.

Friday morning, she escaped the tour for the morning, along with her two tagalongs, and completed several consecutive dives. The view above the south coast of France was stunning. Sparkling waters of the sea off in the distance. Or was it a lagoon? Green forests and farmland stretched out beneath her. Villages all painted in a similar beige stone color. There was even an above ground aqueduct, set on a massive bridge over the roads and pasture. It was all so beautiful.

Violet remembered her first tandem jump with Nick and the way he'd lost his sense of direction, not recognizing any of the landmarks. She smiled to herself, understanding how he felt. Her stomach fluttered, recalling the sensation of falling through the sky with him, harnessed to him. Yes, even then she was not immune to the attraction, despite being angry with him at the time. She sighed as she focused again on aiming for her landing spot. What was she going to do about him?

Late that night, after a long afternoon of sightseeing, Amelia approached Violet with her tablet. Breanna and Lilly were on the screen.

"Hello, girls." Violet waved, happy to see them.

"Don't get too excited," Bree said with a slight frown. "This is an intervention."

Violet's gaze swerved to Amelia, who nodded firmly at her.

"Why?" Violet dragged the word out.

Amelia put a hand on her arm. "Because we all think you need to fix things up with Nick."

Annoyance rose. "Well, I think it is none of your business. Any of you." Tiredness pulled at her—perhaps she was still a little jet lagged. She was not in the mood.

"Too bad." Lilly waggled a finger. "You need to hear us out."

"Because we love you," Bree said.

"This does not feel like love." Violet grabbed a pillow and hugged it to her chest. "This feels like an ambush."

"Listen," Bree said. "I have never seen a guy look at you like Nick does. He's in love with you. Like, head over heels, smitten."

Violet shifted her gaze to Amelia again, who nodded and smiled. "It's true."

Her heartbeat shifted into overdrive. "Even if you're right, Daddy won't have a bar of it."

"Pfft." This from Lilly. "It's your life. Just look at the guy. Why would you give that up because Daddy says so? I could look at that man's legs all day long."

Bree and Amelia giggled, nodding.

Violet allowed a small smile to escape. "He is pretty cute."

"Yes," Amelia said. "And you are just as besotted with him as he is with you. So call him already." She finished with an emphatic nudge to Violet's shoulder.

"All right. All right." Violet lifted her hands as though to ward them off. "I'll call him."

CHAPTER FOURTEEN

What started as a headache and a sneezy, runny nose had developed into a full-blown flu with fever and hacking cough. Nick had been off work for several days now, keeping to his room most of the time, unwilling to pass this infection onto anyone in the Franklin household.

To make matters worse, Violet had not responded to a single one of his messages, so he was more miserable than before. Although he'd barely touched his phone for the last two days. Couldn't bear the brightness of the screen. Couldn't concentrate on the words and images. All he knew was she wasn't there. Before the gala, they'd been in contact in some form every day. And now, nothing. He felt bereft.

And oh, how he missed his family. Times like these, Mum would nurse him with compassion, take him to the doctor, bring him everything he needed. Not that the Franklin's neglected him, but it wasn't the same. He missed Mum more than ever. And Dad. And his sisters. He'd been too sick to even call them.

Mud had phoned him once, but after a few one-syllable answers, he'd got the message.

"Dude, you don't sound good."

"Nah."

"Get better, mate. Call me when you're up to it."

"K." Nick hadn't even tried to end the call, leaving it to Mud.

On Saturday morning, he finally felt well enough to get out of bed and shower. The fever had subsided, and his body didn't ache all over anymore.

"Look who's risen from the grave." Lexi grinned at him as he exited the bathroom, feeling a little fresher.

"Half risen, maybe," Nick answered, his voice hoarse.

"Well, good to see you're improving." She nodded and went on about her business.

Nick went to the kitchen, poured himself a glass of water, selected a banana, and shuffled back to his room, already tired. After eating the fruit, he was ready for a nap.

He spent most of the day drifting between sleep, nibbling on food, and trying to watch a movie or two. Trying not to think about Violet. Trying not to think about how much he missed her, his mum, his sisters, his dad, Mud. Heck, he even missed the tall termite mounds, the stringy bark gum trees, and the beautiful blue waters of the East Alligator River. Home. He missed home.

Lyn brought him a plate of food in the evening, although his appetite still wasn't great. Even if it was lasagna, one of his favorites. "Thanks Lyn," he mumbled as she put it down next to where he sat on the bed.

"You okay?" She looked at him askance.

"Getting there." With his voice the way it was, he didn't sound convincing.

She gave him a direct look. "No, I mean, are you *okay*?"

Nick lowered his eyes. "Just a bit homesick." Just a lot homesick. And heartsick. And Violet-sick.

"It's hard being unwell so far away from your family, hey?" Lyn's eyes crinkled with compassion.

"Yeah." Nick averted his gaze again.

"Now that you're at least upright, why don't you try giving them a call?"

"I should, eh?" Nick nodded. Although seeing his family might make him feel worse. He picked up his phone, and Lyn left the room. But he paused too long before making the call. His heart would ache more if he spoke to any of them now, so he let the phone slip from his hand.

Instead, he tried to eat some lasagna, swallowed another dose of Tylenol and curled up under the blanket. If he just slept some more, he could avoid this loneliness that threatened to overtake him.

Nick jolted awake to the sound of his ringtone. Groggy, he fumbled with his phone. Precious. It was Violet. He scrambled to get a grip and push the answer button before she gave up.

"Violet." It came out as a squeak, and he tried to clear his throat.

"Hey." Violet sounded hesitant.

"It's good to hear your voice." His heart pounded. She had no idea how good.

"Sorry, did I wake you?" she asked.

"No. Yes. It doesn't matter." What was the time? He glanced at his watch. Only nine o'clock.

"You sound …"

"I've been crook. Sick. Not much voice." He croaked, then coughed for good measure.

"Oh, sorry. I should let you …"

"No. Don't hang up. Please." He sounded desperate, even in his own ears. "How's the tour going?"

A pause. "It's great. The people are lovely. The food is delicious. And the scenery is perfect. You'll be happy to know I've even had some skydiving practice."

This was awkward. She sounded so hesitant. "I'm glad you're enjoying it." *And I wish I was there with you.*

"Listen. I'm sorry I haven't answered your texts. I—"

"It's me who's apologizing here, Violet. I know I hurt you with what I said. I never wanted to make you feel like I looked down on you, because I don't." Nick swallowed. He needed to get this out before he lost his chance. "I … I actually think you're amazing. And you are right. I'm a hypocrite."

"You're no hypocrite, Nick." Violet's response was swift. "I reacted badly and said the first thing that came into my head. As I do." She let out an awkward chuckle. "Because you were right about me acting from my heart. My father has been trying to train me out of that since I was a little girl, and that's why I reacted to you so strongly."

"So … are we good, then? Am I forgiven?" Nick held his breath.

"Yes, you're forgiven."

Nick heard the smile in her voice, and he breathed out in relief. "Thank you. That means a lot."

"You're welcome. But we still have things to talk about." The weight of her words came clearly through the phone.

"Yeah, we do." Nick sighed. "Do you have time? I need to tell you something."

Another pause. "Sure. Let me just find a place to sit."

"Where are you?"

"I was just leaving my hotel room, but I'm going back inside."

"Do you need to go? This can wait." Nick didn't want her to miss her tour or get her in trouble. Besides, he didn't know how long his voice would hold out.

"I don't want to wait. What did you want to say?"

Nick drew in a deep breath and let it out in a puff. "Do you remember when I told you about how I got my nickname, Ned Flanders?"

"Yes. Your friends couldn't get you to do anything immoral or illegal."

"Yeah, but there's more to the story."

"Okay." She drew the word out.

"It was also a time when all my mates were going out with girls, fooling around with them a bit, then breaking up. They would be like, 'hey Nick, you go out with that chick, so her friend has an excuse to go out with me.' That kind of stuff."

"Sounds like typical adolescent boy behavior." Sarcasm laced Violet's voice.

"True. But I noticed those girls crying, hurt by the boys and their behavior, and it hit me hard. I decided I didn't want to be one of those guys who broke a girl's heart through a selfish desire to have some fun. I made a promise to myself that I wouldn't get involved with a girl until I was sure it was going somewhere permanent."

Complete silence. Well, except for the sound of her breath coming through the phone, and his heart beating in his ears.

"You're saying you've never been with a girl?"

"Never."

"Have you kissed a girl?" Violet sounded almost disbelieving.

Nick chuckled softly. "Unless you count silly eight-year-old kisses when I didn't even know what kisses meant."

More silence. What was she thinking? Maybe she didn't believe him. Maybe she thought he was plain crazy. Either way, Nick's heart continued to race out of control.

"Me neither." Her voice was barely above a whisper.

"Pardon." Shock surged through him. Did he hear her right?

"I've never, um, been … kissed."

Delight shot through every part of him. He didn't know what to say.

"I was fixated on Lyall for so long and I thought he would be the one, so I never even looked at anyone else. Then with Alistair, well, he tried to once, but I dodged him. Wasn't feeling it."

Nick laughed. An amazed, astounded laugh, like he'd just hit the jackpot. "I don't know what to say. This is …"

"Yes, it is." Violet giggled. "But I really have to go now, or I'll miss breakfast. We'll talk again soon, alright?"

"Alright."

———

VIOLET LEANED back in her chair. Talk about mind blown. Could this guy get any better? She let out a long breath. Her friends were right. She would be a complete fool not to pursue a relationship with Nick. She'd never met anyone with his level of integrity. What were the chances she'd find someone else like that?

But something he'd said triggered a memory. Something about eight-year-olds and not knowing what kisses meant. Violet had never looked at her memories of Lyall that way. Eight-year-old Lyall was still in that innocent child part of life. He wouldn't have realized the hopes and dreams he'd planted in her as a little girl. All that talk of growing up and marrying her. Why had she believed it and claimed it as an unbreakable promise?

Because you were a little girl desperate for love and acceptance.

The truth dropped into her mind like an unexpected breeze. Even then, she hadn't felt accepted by her parents. Daddy was always cross with her for running up to strangers or giving her toys away to the poor kids she met. She remembered impulsively throwing her arms around her father one day, only to have him push her away with a growl. That rejection had hurt, even though she later learned he was talking to someone important at the time. It didn't matter. The damage was done.

So with no evident love from her father, she'd hung all her hopes on a boy. To the point she neither saw nor heard that he wasn't interested in her in that way.

Violet sighed. What a waste.

But I have loved you with an everlasting love.

Tears pricked her eyes. A verse from the Bible gripped her. Where was that? It was a verse Nick had shared with her one time when she was questioning him. Violet flicked open the notes app on her phone. Oh, yes. Jeremiah thirty-one. *Thank you, Jesus.*

His love had preceded everything and would carry on for eternity. He'd loved that eight-year-old girl, even when she never felt it. Suddenly she saw a picture in her mind of that moment Daddy had pushed her away, but this time she turned and found the arms of Jesus right behind her. Oh, how beautiful. He was there all along, holding her, loving her. Violet closed her eyes to drink in the sensation of peace that flooded her. She was loved. She was accepted.

A knock on her hotel room door jolted her out of her reverie.

"Violet, are you okay?" Amelia poked her head in.

Violet wiped the tears from her cheeks and rose quickly. How long had she been sitting there, soaking in that healing balm? "I'm fine."

"The tour bus is about to leave. You didn't come down to eat."

Violet looked at the time. Goodness. She'd missed breakfast all together. But she didn't care. The lightness winging through her soul was worth a few hunger pains. "Don't worry. I'll grab something from the cafe on the way out."

"Have you been talking to Nick this whole time?" Amelia asked as they hurried down the hallway.

"No. He got me thinking. That's all. And then I was kind of praying, I guess." Violet was unsure how to explain it to someone who didn't have her faith yet.

"But you two made up, right?"

Violet giggled. "Yes, we made up." And she couldn't wait to talk to him again. The next chance she would get to call him would be late that night, which would be the middle of the afternoon for him. That might work if he was still home recovering. But it seemed like an eternity away.

"Yay." Amelia clapped.

Violet stopped walking abruptly and turned to Amelia, the memory of her experience that morning taking over again. "I need to tell you something."

Amelia laughed. "Did he propose already?"

"What? Over the phone? No. Of course not." Violet shook her head, though the idea made her heart skip a beat.

Her friend frowned. "What, then?"

"I … I had this realization this morning, and I know it is true for you, too." She looked directly into Amelia's eyes. "Jesus loves you. It's important for me to tell you that. He's loved you since before you were born and will love you forever, regardless of whether you return that love."

"Wow." Amelia giggled, then sobered. "Okay. Thanks, I guess."

"Just promise me you'll think about what I said. And feel free to ask me about it at any time."

Amelia seemed a little unsure but agreed anyway. "Can we go to the bus now?"

Violet laughed then. "Sure, let's go."

They spent the day sightseeing around Marseille and on a cruise to the Calanques National Park. Ancient buildings, stunning views, and crystal-clear turquoise waters ensured a spectacular day. In between writing copious notes on the service, staff, and experiences, Violet sent photos of some of the best views to Nick. In return, he sent her photos of his pillow, two Tylenol, and a jealous GIF, all of which made her smile.

She had to drag her attention away from the phone again to interact with other tour guests. Violet needed to gauge their satisfaction with the tour without them realizing she was critiquing the company. Amelia and Drew, always nearby, could sit back and enjoy the tour, although Amelia also engaged with other passengers. She'd relate her findings to Violet that evening.

So she couldn't call Nick again until late. She found her heart pounding as she pressed the dial button, and her breath caught as he answered.

"G'day." Nick was still croaky.

"Hey."

"Hi." A chuckle.

Violet giggled. "How are you feeling today?"

"Much better for talking to you."

That husky voice was going to undo her. She laughed nervously again, then swallowed. "Um … I wanted to tell you I called things off with Alistair last week."

Silence except for the sound of his breath coming through the phone. What was he thinking? Her nerves catapulted, but she needed him to know how she felt.

"And, well, at the gala, I didn't really mean maybe … about you."

"Violet—"

"The truth is I felt it too." She wasn't ready to hear any objections. "Back in Australia last year. Did you know I keep a journal?"

"You do?"

"Yes. And I've gone back and reread my entry for that day a hundred times. How much do you remember?" Now that she was committed, her nerves settled somewhat.

"Pretty much all of it."

"Do you remember helping me step down from that tiny aircraft after the scenic flight?"

A breath. "I remember. That was when I first thought we could have something more than a passing acquaintance."

"Me too. I wrote about that moment, in detail. But I was confused. Vulnerable. It was two days out from learning Lyall didn't want me. I didn't trust myself. And then I came home, and Daddy was upset with me and my lack of good judgement where TESView was concerned." Violet let out a regretful laugh. "I went back and scrawled nasty things on that page of my journal."

"About me being an unforgivable villain?" Amusement laced Nick's words.

"Kind of."

"And now?"

Nick wasn't about to let her off easy. He wanted to hear it. He deserved to hear it. Violet drew in a deep breath, shoring up her courage. "I haven't been able to stop thinking about you since you arrived in Trinity Lakes. Can we start again? Try exploring this together?"

A shuddering breath came through the phone. "There's nothing I'd like more." He paused. "But … I hate to ask … what about your father?"

A relevant question. Violet's heart sank a little. "What did he say to you?"

"You know about that?"

"He told me." Violet said, then corrected herself. "Well, he implied it."

"He basically warned me off." Nick's voice was flat. "He will make our lives difficult, Vi."

Violet gritted her teeth. Daddy's power plays were more than frustrating. Yet she was ready to fight for this. Nick was far too important for her to quit. "I'll work on him, Nick. And if I have to, I will defy him."

"That means a lot, Vi. More than I can say. But I would rather have his blessing."

Violet frowned. "What are you saying?"

Nick paused. "I'm saying, let's take this slowly. Until your dad eases up, let's just be … um … special friends."

"Special friends? That sounds so corny." But so like him.

"Okay. Extra special friends, then."

Violet laughed. "Fine. If we must."

"Great. I can't wait to see you again."

"Me either."

Another pause. "Violet, I would love to pray about this together. Is that okay?"

Violet jolted. Mind blown again. He valued their relationship so much that he wanted to bring it to Jesus? "Absolutely."

And he did. Nick placed their future in the Lord's hands and prayed her father would soften toward him and their relationship. It was well past midnight before she could put the phone down, both of them saying goodbye for at least an hour and arguing over who was going to hang up first. As if they hadn't planned to talk the very next day. Violet's heart hummed with delight as she fell asleep.

She had a boyfriend.

An amazing boyfriend.

Well, an extra special friend.

CHAPTER FIFTEEN

Although Nick was back at work and finally able to complete the tasks he'd promised Pastor Ladan, the sense of homesickness refused to leave. He ached for his family. He ached for the familiar landscape of home. He even ached for Mud's company. With the time difference, it made it difficult to have regular conversations with any of them. It was either the middle of the night or the middle of the day in Australia when he was free to call.

It was even hard keeping in contact with Violet, though the time difference with France wasn't as bad. She basically had to call him before breakfast every morning, which was around his bedtime. But those conversations were the best. They'd talked through so many things and prayed together every day. Nick was careful not to take a single step without prayerful consideration, and Violet was gratefully on board. More than on board. She said it made her feel secure, knowing Nick was giving the Lord the lead.

It seemed like every time he spoke to her, his heart fell a little deeper. He couldn't wait to tell her everything he felt for her, to hold her in his arms. That longing increased every day. *Lord, please soften Mr. Reynolds's heart.*

Now Violet was due back in America. Nick had wanted to meet her at the airport, but she'd asked him not to.

"I don't want to get Daddy offside before I've talked to him. You understand?"

Yes, Nick understood. He didn't want to drive a further wedge between father and daughter. But it meant he had to wait to see her until she was ready. And waiting was hard.

Monday morning, Nick was supposed to be at the airfield, but a strong wind blew and a storm was expected late morning, so Freefall Adventures canceled all jumps for the day. Left to twiddle his thumbs and wondering how to distract himself from his lonely feelings, Nick considered going down to the church and doing more odd jobs. Or he could go outside and weed the college gardens.

As he pulled his boots on, the rumble of a big motor outside caught his attention. The motor cut out and soon came a knock on the door.

"Coming," he called. The others had already gone off to work, so it fell to him to see who it was.

He swung the door open, still hopping on one foot as he tried to get his foot into the second boot, then did a double take. "Violet?"

There she stood, a cowboy hat on her head, plaid shirt, denim shorts, gorgeous legs, and cowboy boots on her feet. He blew out a long breath. He was unprepared for the impact. Wanted to wrap her in an embrace. Wanted to kiss the life out of her.

"You're not happy to see me?" Violet grinned, although there was a little uncertainty in her eyes.

"More than happy." Nick swallowed. "But you're not making this easy for me looking as gorgeous as that."

She bit her lip alluringly. "Should I go change into a potato sack?"

Nick ran a hand over his face. Lord, help him. "Not sure that would make much difference." He laughed self-consciously.

"I'm here to take you out on a friends' date, seeing as we can't sky-dive today." Violet held up the car keys and jingled them.

Nick looked past her to the four-wheel-drive parked nearby. He didn't recognize the vehicle and there were no other passengers in it. "Where's Drew?"

"I've ditched him." A hardness flashed in her eyes. "I'll tell you all about it later."

"Where are we going?"

"It's a surprise."

"Right. Do I need to bring anything?"

Violet looked him up and down brazenly. "You look mighty fine to me." She turned towards the four-wheeler and then swung back. "You will need your driver's license."

Nick's brain turned to mush at her flirty behavior. "Why?"

"Because you're driving."

"So, what's this all about?" Nick asked once they were on the road, heading out of town.

"A little birdy told me you were homesick, so we're going off-road. I know that's something you love to do back home. I was planning for another day, but since everything was called off today, I brought it forward."

Nick's heart thudded at her thoughtfulness. "What little birdy told you I was homesick?"

"Well, you actually."

"I never said—"

"All those silly GIFs with someone singing "All By Myself," the photo of you on your own in the Bellbird Café? You did so say."

Nick laughed self-consciously. "I guess I did."

"So we are going to have an Australiana day. As much as we can."

His heart swelled again. "Thank you." He reached over and took her hand in his, threading their fingers together. And it felt like home.

Violet glanced at their hands and back at him.

"Extra-special friends." He winked. Her face lit up with a wide smile. "I didn't know you had a four-wheel drive."

"I don't." Violet shrugged. "I borrowed it from a friend. And before you ask, he's happy for you to be driving it."

Nick's excitement grew at the thought of being away from the town and out into nature. "So where we are going? Does it have river crossings?"

Violet laughed. "I doubt it. It's probably tame compared to what you're used to. We'd have to go a lot further into the mountains to find the really rough trails."

"I can deal with tame." Nick had to release her hand to shift gears as they turned off the main highway toward the mountains.

Violet's predictions of a tame road were accurate. More like a gravel dirt road than the off-road trails he was used to, but Nick found a less-used track off to the side. Violet squealed as he veered onto it. Rain had washed out parts of the track, leaving it rutted, making for a slow, jagged ride. Violet held on tight as the vehicle lurched and swayed, but she still grinned and even laughed.

"You don't mind me going off off-road?"

"Not at all. This is great fun." The last word came out like a groan as she fell against the door when the four-wheeler dipped into a deep pothole. But then she laughed again. "Way better than a roller coaster."

"Agreed." Nick grinned. "You should be close to doing your assessment dive, yeah?"

Violet nodded. "Most likely in the next week."

"How are you feeling about it?"

"Confident. Nervous."

"You'll be fine." He squeezed her hand. "We'll have to go out and celebrate after."

"Another friend date?" She clapped her hands together. "I like the sound of that. What will we do?"

"Leave it to me." It didn't matter what or where. Being near her was enough.

Soon they arrived at a grassy ridge overlooking a pine-covered valley with more mountains in the distance, and Nick pulled the truck to a stop. They got out to enjoy the view, and Violet took several photos. She even took a selfie of them together with the stunning scenery in the background, although the wind whipping their hair around their faces made it difficult.

"This is going on my socials as soon as we're back in range," she said.

"Are you sure?" Nick remembered the gossip that started last time images of them circulated.

"I'm sure." She nodded, and that hard look flashed in her eyes again. "Listen. I have some things to tell you. But first, a surprise."

That wide smile lit up her face, the smile that made his insides turn to water every time. She jogged back to the car and opened the back. Inside was an esky—cooler—and a picnic rug. Violet grabbed the blanket and asked him to bring the esky.

"What have we got here?" Nick played along.

Violet spread the picnic blanket on the grass, and they sat down together. She motioned for him to open the cooler, her eyes sparkling as she leaned back on her elbows, legs stretched out before her. As Nick lifted the lid, something sprang out at him. He yelped and fell back. Violet's laughter echoed from the hills around them as he straightened. A spring-loaded snake lay by his knees.

"Revenge, is it?" His lips twisted, trying to hold back his own laughter. Truth be told, he could kiss her right now. How easy it would be. Instead, he picked up the fake snake and tossed it at her.

"And so worth it." She wore a smug grin.

"You'll keep." A warning he would find a way to pay her back. This could be a fun pastime, playing pranks on each other.

He turned his attention back to the esky. Precious. There were several cartons of the Northern Territory iced coffee he loved. He picked one up and looked at Violet, confounded. "But how…?"

The self-satisfied smile spread. "I have several contacts in the travel industry, you know. It took multiple flights and lots of juggling, but I wanted you to have something from home."

Nick didn't know what to say. She'd gone to all that trouble for him. Was it possible she cared as much for him as he did for her?

"There's more." She waved a hand toward the esky.

Nick peeked into the cooler. Two portions of vanilla slice and a packet of Tim Tams. How perfectly Australian. "Are you going to join me for this treat?"

"Of course I am." She reached toward him. "Hand it over."

Once they were settled with their snacks, Nick turned to her again. "What did you want to tell me about?"

———

VIOLET LOOKED DOWN at the chocolate-coated cookie melting in her fingers. She shook her head. The things she had learned since arriving home. Anger churned deep within. A gust of wind blew strands of hair across her mouth and she dragged them off.

"Daddy fired Tony."

Nick's head jerked back. "What?"

Violet nodded. "The same day he sent me to France and steamrolled you. Although he implied Tony had resigned. I can't believe he'd do that."

"But why?" Nick's brows furrowed.

"I caught up with Tony in church yesterday. He didn't want to say anything at first, but I coaxed it out of him."

"Meaning you charmed it out of him." Nick shook his head with a half-smile.

"Sure." Violet let out a short laugh. "Anyway, apparently Daddy fired him because he failed to keep you away from me."

Nick's head dropped, and he groaned. Then he reached toward her and squeezed her hand. "I'm sorry. I've caused you so much trouble. You were close to Tony, weren't you?"

Violet sighed. It was good to talk about these things, to have an ear that understood. "I still am, but I miss having him around."

Nick shook his head, stood to his feet, and paced back and forth a little. "This is all my fault. I should have—"

"No, Nick." Violet wasn't about to let him wear this. "This is Daddy's problem. He has to learn he can't force me to be the person he wants me to be. He can't send me overseas every time he doesn't like what I'm doing, or keep me here if I make mistakes."

Nick sat down again, although he still wore a troubled look. "Have you spoken to him about it?"

"Not since he put me on a plane to Nice. Our last conversation didn't end well."

"What are you going to do?"

"Right now, I'm too angry to talk to him. I just want to get on with my life and live it the way I choose."

Nick sighed. "You know that's not the way we're going to get past this." Compassion filled his eyes, despite the challenge in his words.

Tears rose and spilled over onto her cheeks, and her lips trembled. "All I want is for us to be together. To be happy."

Nick reached over and brushed her tears away gently with his thumb. "Me too. But I also know you love your father. You'll never be content while he is unhappy with you."

Violet covered her face with her hands as the tears flowed more freely. How right Nick was. She hated being at odds with Daddy. She just wished he'd see Nick the same way she did. Nick brushed against her as he moved beside her and slipped an arm around her shoulders, and she leaned into him. "Why does this have to be so hard?"

Nick didn't answer for a moment, although he did let out a grunt. "I don't know. But I think it's worth working through." His arm squeezed tighter and his voice thickened. "You're worth a bit of hardship, Vi."

She pulled back from him to look into his eyes, though her face must be a mess. A gentle smile lit his eyes. How blessed was she to have this man here? "I think I love you."

Nick's Adam's apple bobbed as he swallowed and his eyes traveled to her lips. Then he chuckled, brushing her hair away from her face. "I know I love you."

Violet's heart surged at the tenderness in his gaze. He was right. This was definitely worth some hardship. "And we're going to sort this thing out with Daddy first."

Nick sighed. "That's what the Lord would want." He shifted away from her, breaking the spell. "But we should head back before the storm breaks." He jerked his chin toward the horizon, where heavy clouds gathered. "Or before the temptation to take advantage of this moment becomes too much."

Violet giggled at his insinuation. "Is that right?" She got up to gather their things and continued in a sing-song voice. "You want to kiss me. You want to kiss me."

"You have no idea." He laughed as he lifted the cooler into the truck.

Back on the road, Violet couldn't get their conversation out of her head. He loved her. And she'd told him she loved him. It was true. Everything about Nick blew her away, and she couldn't imagine wanting to be with anyone else. Ever.

"Where to next?" Nick brought her back to the present.

She cleared her throat, pushing her swelling emotions aside. "We could have a late lunch at the Bellbird Café. I'm sure you'd enjoy one of those meat pies you always talk about. Then I'll take you to the Trinity Lakes Historical Museum—it reopened recently. They have an entire section on Australia in there. I went to the grand opening. It was great."

"True? Sounds awesome."

"You may know the girl who runs it. Eloise Reilly? You would have seen her at Trinity Life, I'm certain."

Nick's lips thinned into a straight line. "To be honest, I haven't tried to get to know anyone there. Not until the last couple of weeks, anyway." He scratched his chin, clearly self-conscious. "I didn't really want to be there. Wanted to be back at the Community Church—where you were—so I kind of avoided any connection or involvement. But maybe I'll recognize her."

When they entered the museum, he nodded when he saw the young woman Violet pointed out. "Oh, Ellie. Yes, I've met her."

They went over and greeted her.

"I hope you enjoy your visit." Ellie reached into a cupboard nearby. "Here, I have a secret stash." She opened a tin toward Nick and revealed some Anzac biscuits.

"Nice." Nick reached for one, then Ellie offered one to Violet.

"No, thank you. I ate plenty for lunch." She patted her stomach for emphasis.

Ellie looked from her to Nick and back. "So you two are…?"

"Just friends," they answered in unison, then laughed.

Although anyone with eyes in their head could tell they were so much more.

———

Just as Violet promised, the Australian section of the museum was full of familiar memorabilia and history that made him feel a little at home. He learned about the Australian history within Trinity Lakes, how an abandoned child, first housed at the present Bible College, was raised by Australian relatives, returned to Trinity Lakes as an adult, and turned the orphanage into a Bible College.

"Wow. That's amazing."

"Isn't it?" Violet agreed.

Nick turned and watched a video on the annual Anzac Day footy game the locals played in Trinity Lakes.

"Pity I was here too late for the game," he murmured.

Violet closed the gap between them and slipped her hand into his. "Maybe next year."

The breath left him. Next year. Would he be staying? He was still not one hundred percent sure. But he squeezed her hand. "Maybe next year."

"Oh, come here." Violet tugged his hand and led him over to a costume section. They spent several minutes dressing in different historical items and taking selfies together, laughing and acting out characters from times past.

Just as he removed an Abraham Lincoln hat and beard, a man walked up to Violet.

"Hey, gorgeous," the man said in a suave voice. Nick studied him, trying to keep calm. High-end suit. Debonair stance. Air of superiority. This must be Alistair, the ex-boyfriend.

Violet seemed as shocked as he was. "Alistair? What are you doing here?"

"I've come to take you to dinner, of course." He flashed a

thousand-dollar smile. Nick wondered if that's how much he paid to get teeth that white.

"No, I mean, what are you doing *here*?" She gestured to the surrounding building, eyes sparking. "How did you find me?"

Anger churned in Nick. Was her father that controlling? He suspected the man had sent Alistair after her. But challenging Alistair in a public place would not end well. He tugged at Violet's elbow. "Just go with him."

Her head jerked around, eyes wide in disbelief, and she opened her mouth to protest.

"There is no sense in making a scene. We'll sort it out. Remember, we're trusting the Lord with this." Much harder to do than say. Nick would rather tell Alistair how things stood. But this wasn't the time or the place.

Violet stared at him for a moment, then nodded, put down the dress-ups she held, and followed Alistair out the door.

CHAPTER SIXTEEN

Violet fumed. As soon as she got him out the door, she was going to give Alistair a piece of her mind. How dare he interrupt her time with Nick? And after she had clearly told him she didn't want to pursue a relationship with him. Thank goodness for Nick's level-headed warning to keep a civil tongue in public.

However, outside the doors, instead of an empty street, Violet recognized Selena from the Trinity Lakes Gazette with her camera. Before she could even open her mouth, the camera flashed in Violet's eyes. "Really?" What was going on?

Alistair slid an arm around her waist and pulled her to his side. Violet jerked her chin around to see he was grinning and posing for Selena. Did he set this up? What was he trying to achieve?

Numbed by shock, it took her several breaths to realize Alistair was answering questions, telling Selena and anyone within earshot of an imminent announcement. He even had the audacity to lean down and kiss her possessively on the forehead. Heavy drops of rain chose that moment to fall from the thick clouds, giving her a good excuse for an escape.

Violet roughly pulled away from Alistair and headed for the parking lot. Oh, but Nick had the keys to the truck. She looked over her shoulder to see if he had emerged from the museum. Instead, she could only see Selena following her, pressing her with questions about Alistair, who was also close on her heels.

"You have got to be kidding me," she mumbled under her breath. What was she going to do?

Drew leaned against the Mercedes a short distance away. Too bad if he'd driven Alistair here. Now Drew could drive her home. Right now. She jogged to the car and slid in quickly, thankful Drew had seen her coming and was already in the driver's seat.

"Get me out of here, Drew."

"Sure. I'm just waiting for Mr. Harrington to catch up."

"You had better not be behind this, Drew," she muttered.

"I'm only following orders."

The passenger door opened and Alistair jumped in.

Following orders? Drew worked for Daddy. Violet's stomach clenched. She turned on Alistair as they pulled away from the curb. "How dare you ambush me like that?" Her voice came out way louder than she expected, but she was too incensed to care.

"Calm down, Violet. You know how I feel about you." Alistair flicked her a smooth grin.

"And I told you I am not interested." Still loud, still high-pitched. She was nowhere near calming down.

"You haven't even given us a chance."

"So you thought you could force my hand by making a public display?" *Breathe, Violet. Breathe.*

Alistair shrugged. "You wouldn't risk causing a scandal."

Of all the arrogant …

"It turns out I don't care about what people think as much as you believe. It's my father who worries about that. Was this his idea?"

The smirk vanished from Alistair's face, and he turned away

from her. "He thinks—we both think—you and I would be good together. He only wants what's best for you."

Violet folded her arms across her chest, wild fury subsiding into a seething cauldron. "You mean what's best for The Reynolds Group. Deny it if you will."

Alistair shifted in his seat. "I won't deny that our union would benefit both companies, but that's not the only reason I want you." He reached out the brush stray hairs back from her face.

Violet felt sick and pushed his hand away. "Right. So what are the other reasons?"

"Just look at you. Beautiful. Stylish. Clever …"

Shallow. Shallow. Shallow. Nothing like the way Nick spoke to her. Poor Nick. She wondered how he was taking this. Ambushed in a community museum, of all places. Violet shook her head.

"How did you know we were at the museum?"

"What do you mean?" Alistair hedged.

"I mean, how did you know we were at the museum? I didn't tell a soul where I was going today."

Silence. He tugged at his seatbelt, then tightened it again.

"Alistair?"

"He's only trying to protect you," he finally said in a small voice.

"You mean Daddy?"

Guilty might as well have appeared in large capital letters on his forehead. "He's been tracking your phone since you broke off with me."

Violet clenched her fists. Why couldn't Daddy leave her alone and let her live her life? He was getting worse and worse. "Do neither of you see how this could be construed as an invasion of privacy? For me and for Nick."

"Like I said, he's only trying to—"

"Save it, Alistair."

Drew pulled the car into the driveway, and Violet couldn't get out quick enough, despite the rain now falling heavily.

"Drew, take Alistair wherever he's going."

But Alistair followed her out of the Mercedes. "Your father invited me to stay in the guest house."

"Here?" Violet's voice squeaked as her blood boiled again. "You're staying here? No, no, no. You can't." Even though the guest house wasn't part of the main building, it was too close for her comfort.

Alistair smirked at her. "It is Mr. Reynold's house, is it not?"

Violet shook her head and ducked for cover in the portico. The noose was tightening around her neck. Well, she wouldn't cave. She pulled out her phone and shot a quick text to Amelia. Then she turned to Drew, who had finished parking the car and now jogged toward them. "I'll need you to take me out again, Drew. Give me five minutes."

Violet glared at Alistair as she dashed past. Inside, she raced to her room and repacked the suitcase she'd only just emptied. She was not staying under the same roof as Alistair. Not even on the same property. Who knew what he had planned? The mere fact he was staying would start the tongues wagging.

On the way downstairs, she ducked into her office and grabbed all her current files, along with her laptop. Who knew how long Alistair would hang around? Laden with her bags, equipment, and umbrella, she headed back outside. Alistair still loitered.

Ignoring him, she addressed Drew. "Can you open the trunk for me, please?"

Drew pressed a button on the remote and helped load her things.

"Where are you going?" Alistair asked. Of course.

"Away from you." Violet was not in the mood to be polite as she brushed past him and slid into the front seat of the car.

"I don't think your father will be happy about that."

Violet pressed her lips together and shook her head. "I don't actually care. Unlike you, I am not his puppet." Not anymore, anyway. With that, she shut the door and glanced across at Drew. "Take me to Amelia's."

Drew was silent on the brief drive. Violet hoped he regretted being involved in the setup. When they arrived at her friend's flat, he helped her take her things inside.

"You might as well go back and look after Alistair." She sighed. "I'll be fine here tonight."

Drew seemed to be in two minds. He was probably under strict instructions not to let her out of his sight, but Amelia wasn't about to let him into her tiny unit. Violet alone would make it cramped enough. For a moment, she thought he might sit in his car all night, but he eventually drove away.

"All right now." Amelia sat down with her, having already made coffee for them both. "Tell me all about it."

Violet launched into an animated diatribe over the events of the afternoon, finishing with her declaration that she would not stay in her home whilst Alistair was hovering about. Letting out a long breath, she realized Amelia looked uncomfortable. Violet reached out and put a hand on Amelia's knee. "Don't worry. I won't stay here. I'll go to the Lakeview Inn. Coming here was more of a decoy."

"It's not that I don't want you here …"

"I know. You don't have the space." Violet knew the truth— Amelia feared the repercussions of assisting her. Amelia had a healthy awe of the powerful Morgan Reynolds. Or perhaps unhealthy.

"But what you're going through sounds awful." Amelia groaned. "Especially when things are finally going well with Nick."

Nick. Her heart leaped at just hearing his name. "Yes. So well." Troubles momentarily forgotten, she grinned at Amelia. "He told me he loves me."

"Oh, that's amazing." Amelia threw her arms around Violet. "I'm so happy for you."

"Me too." Violet grabbed her phone and pulled up the photos they'd taken together. She handed the phone to Amelia to see, and a thought struck her. Perhaps she should launch her own media campaign about her love life—one telling a story contrary to the one Daddy and Alistair were trying to construct. But first …

"Do you know how to tell if there's a tracking device on my phone? Daddy must have put something on there a couple of weeks ago."

"Sure, I can have a look." Amelia tapped away for a few seconds. "Yeah, it's easy enough. He's just downloaded an app. Do you want me to remove it?"

"Yes please. And can you put a new password on the phone so it can't happen again?" Violet breathed out. At least she could cut one tie tonight.

———

I'm so sorry, Nick.

It was late when the text came through from Violet. He'd left the museum, head reeling, to see her taking off down the street while a journalist gave chase. Thankfully, she'd made it safely to the Mercedes with Drew and escaped. Not knowing what he was supposed to do with the four-by-four, he drove it back to the Bible College and spent the next few hours pacing the kitchen, the living room, his bedroom. He couldn't sit still, but he prayed. He prayed a lot.

Apart from sending her a message to ask if she was okay, he'd left her alone, not wanting to interrupt whatever she was sorting out. And she hadn't answered him until now.

Can you talk?

In response, his phone burst into melody.

"G'day," he answered.

"Hey."

"What happened, Vi?"

There was silence for a few seconds and then sounds he figured were sniffles. Precious. She was crying. "Vi? Are you okay?" He hated not being right with her, to comfort her.

"It's all Daddy's doing." Her voice croaked.

"I figured as much."

Another sniff. "He's always been overprotective, but this is getting ridiculous."

Nick sighed. "Dads can get a bit crazy when they think they're losing their daughters."

"That doesn't make it right."

"No, it doesn't."

"And he has more chance of losing me by trying to force my hand."

"True. Have you spoken to him?"

"Not yet. I'm even less ready to talk to him now. Although Alistair probably has, which means Daddy will call me before long." Violet groaned. "What am I going to say to him?"

"All I can say is to be honest with him. Tell him how all this makes you feel."

"I'm not sure he's going to listen."

"Well, we can pray that he does." Words of wisdom, maybe, but on the inside, Nick struggled to maintain his own composure.

"Can you pray with me, Nick?"

"Of course." His throat clogged. Violet seemed to have so much faith and trust in him, while Nick's doubts fought to take hold. But pray with her he did, that the Lord would soften Morgan Reynolds's heart toward both of them.

"What's next, Vi? Is there anything I can do?" he asked as they finished praying.

Violet breathed out a long sigh. "I'll be staying at the Lakeview Inn for the next few nights. I've organized Tony to keep an eye on things for me, but can you bring the truck around here in the morning? My friend says I can hang onto it for a little longer."

"Sure. I'll come around first thing." Any excuse to see her was good for him.

"If you come early enough, you can join me for breakfast."

Nick could hear the smile in her voice. At least that hadn't changed. She still wanted to be with him, despite the obstacles.

"Are you asking me on a date?" He couldn't keep the grin from his face.

"A friend date." Violet giggled.

Thank goodness the tension eased as they bantered for several minutes before reluctantly ending the call. Morning would come soon enough.

Arriving at the Lakeview Inn, he discovered Tony in the parking lot, apparently waiting for him. Nick's stomach clenched. Would Tony be bitter, since Nick was the reason he lost his job? He approached Tony cautiously, trying to offer a friendly smile.

"G'day, mate."

Relief flooded him as Tony met his greeting with a solid handshake and a thump on the back.

"Good to see you, Nick."

"I'm sorry you lost your job, Tony." Nick squinted in the bright morning sunshine.

"This is not on you." Tony shook his head. "It's Mr. Reynolds who has the problem. And while I regret being dismissed, I do not regret telling Mr. Reynolds a few home truths. I've got your back, man." Tony gripped his shoulder.

"Wow." Gratitude caught in Nick's throat. "Thanks, mate. It means a lot." More than he could say, in this environment where the rich and powerful were all against him.

"You're more than welcome. Now, can I have those keys? I

am tasked with taking Amelia to the Trinity Lakes Gazette office to try to talk some sense into Selena."

"Of course, yes." Nick dropped the keys into his hand. "All the best with that."

"I'm sure it'll be fine. I'll be back in an hour to take you wherever you need to go."

"Great. Thanks, Tony."

Tony gave him a salute. "Now get in there. She's waiting in the dining room."

Nick needed no more encouragement. He took the steps to the veranda two at a time and entered the bed-and-breakfast seconds later. His heart leaped a thousand feet in the air, as it did every time he laid eyes on Violet, who was sitting at the dining table, perusing her phone.

Her face lit up as her gazed lifted to his. "Good morning."

How good would it be to receive a greeting like that every morning? And to be able to return it with a tender kiss.

"Hey" was the only word that passed his lips. For now, that had to be enough. Although … he reached out to squeeze her hand as he sat beside her.

"How are you doing this morning?"

"Not too bad," she replied. "As long as I keep my mind off Daddy, I'm okay."

"Has he called you yet?"

"No, and I'm grateful for that."

"Have you worked out what you'll say to him?"

"Not exactly. But I know I have to hold my ground, whatever he says."

A young woman entered the room with steaming cups of coffee and set them on the table in front of them.

"Nick," Violet said, "This is Tabby. She runs the Inn. I've been filling her in on why I'm here."

Nick widened his eyes at Violet in question. He'd thought she'd want to keep this as quiet as possible.

"Tabby knows I have a home within ten minutes' drive, so it made sense to let her know. Besides, Tabby won't tell a soul."

"Correct." Tabby made a zipping motion over her lips. "Nice to meet you, Nick."

"And you, Tabby."

"I hope everything works out for you both. I'll get your breakfasts."

"Thanks, Tabby." Violet smiled.

Soon, they were tucking into a cooked breakfast of bacon, eggs, and hash browns. "So good," Nick commented between mouthfuls.

"Tabby's a fantastic cook."

"What are you up to today?"

"I'll be following up on the French tour, working on a couple of recommendations. My usual work. What about you?"

"I'm off to the airfield. Ground control today."

"Good thing the weather has cleared."

"Yeah. When is your assessment dive booked?"

"Friday. Will you be there?"

"I wouldn't miss it for the world." Their eyes locked as he grinned at her.

Violet's phone rang, breaking the moment. "I'd better take this. It's Amelia."

She didn't move away as she answered, which struck Nick as significant. He was now part of her trusted inner circle. Her trust meant more to him than he could say. After a few yesses, okays, and a big thank you, Violet ended the call and picked up her fork again. "Thank goodness that's sorted." She looked at him and gave a deep sigh.

"The Gazette?"

"Yes. Selena is zealous about publishing the truth. So when Amelia explained the story Daddy's people told her wasn't the truth, she was happy to hold off publishing. Amelia even showed her some photos of you and me together. But Selena asked if she could publish the true story when it is safe to do so. Amelia agreed on my behalf. I hope that's okay with you."

"If that truth is that we are together with at least your daddy's acceptance, then I would be happy to declare it to the world." Nick squeezed her hand again. Oh, how he prayed that would be the outcome.

Violet squeezed his hand in return, her eyes filling with longing as they drifted to his lips. "This is so hard, isn't it?"

"It really is." Nick laughed softly and scratched at his beard. "And it's probably at this point I need to leave and go to work."

CHAPTER SEVENTEEN

Only a few minutes after Nick left, Violet's phone rang again. Daddy. Hurrying back to her room, she closed the door before answering.

"What are you doing, sweet pea?"

Not a "hello". No "how are you?" Just an exasperated tone coming through the earpiece. Violet stiffened.

"The real question is, what are *you* doing, Daddy? Spying on me. Tracking me. Sending the press after me."

"I'm trying to protect my little girl. Trying to stop her from making the biggest mistake of her life." His voice sounded thick. Did he actually believe what he said?

Violet bit down on her lip as tears sprang to her eyes. "Daddy, I'm not that little girl anymore. The girl who unwittingly threw herself into the path of danger. You've taught me to be cautious. Maybe too cautious. But I know what I'm doing."

"Do you? Do you really, Violet?"

"It may not look like it to you, because you see me through the lens of what you want me to be. And I am not that woman. I doubt I ever will be." Would he hear her? Really hear her? She held her breath.

"What are you talking about?"

"The sophisticated and cool-headed businesswoman. That's not me."

"That is exactly who you are."

"No. That is who you tried to train me to be. I have never been comfortable in that role."

Silence for a moment. "You'll grow into it. You're still young, sweet pea."

"I highly doubt that, Daddy. I'm creative. I'm messy. I'm emotional. I want to help people, not build an empire."

Silence again. "I see. That boy has poisoned your mind."

Violet groaned inwardly and shook her head. "Nick has nothing to do with it. You said yourself—I've always been emotional. Now I'm learning about how God created me."

A scornful laugh. "So he's brainwashed you, too."

"No, he ha— "

"You and Alistair will make an amazing power couple. The sooner you realize that, the better." Daddy's voice held that no-nonsense tone. He'd shut down, and there would be no point arguing further. Yet she held on.

"No, we wouldn't. And I don't want to be half of a power couple."

"I want you to go back to the house." Firm and resolved.

"Not while Alistair is staying there. You can't force me."

"I can stop paying you."

Wow. Okay. He was losing it. Violet bit her lip again and willed her voice to be steady. "Really, Daddy? I can see the headlines now. 'Business tycoon abandons his daughter.'" If he could use strong-arm business tactics, she could remind him of the scandal-hungry media hovering at his door.

A longer silence this time. Then a deep sigh. "I'm sorry Violet. I wouldn't do that to you. But please go home. I'll ask Alistair to go to a hotel."

Really? She'd actually won an argument—well, part of it? She almost laughed. Perhaps there was hope.

"And give him a chance. Hear him out."

She shook her head. Maybe it was too early to hope. "Okay. But you have to stop tracking my every move."

"Fine."

"Good."

"Good."

"I'll talk to you later."

"Yes. Goodbye."

There was no warmth in their goodbye. This was far from over. Violet sat on the bed, digesting the conversation for a long while. At least she had gained a little ground by standing up to him. *Thank you, Lord.* She prayed she could remain calm dealing with him in future conversations, prayed she could make further headway. *Soften his heart, Jesus.*

A FEW DAYS LATER, Violet sat in the open door of the Cessna, ready to complete her assessment dive. Nick was on the ground, waiting for her, and had prayed with her before taking off. She was so grateful for his support. And not just with skydiving. He'd taken the news of her talk with Daddy in his stride. He'd encouraged her. He'd understood she would need to spend time with Alistair, though she was sure he didn't like it. For good reason, too. Alistair was pushier than ever.

She'd agreed to have lunch with him, and while she didn't want to be seen with him in public, that was preferable to being alone with him. So they agreed to meet at the Country Club Restaurant, insisting that Drew accompany them. Of course, Alistair had lavished her with the most expensive items on the menu and apologized profusely for his involvement in the museum and journalist incident.

"But it's because I … I'm not ready to give up on us."

"You're not ready, or my father's not ready?" Violet couldn't help feeling cynical.

Alistair's eyes dropped to the table momentarily, then raised them again. His gaze swerved to Drew, who sat at a table close by, then dropped his voice. "It's not just him. I think we have something special."

Violet opened her mouth to question him, but he raised a hand to halt her speech.

"Remember that night I cooked for you?"

"Yes." The night he'd tried to move too fast.

"Didn't you feel the chemistry between us? I certainly did."

He reached across the table and squeezed her hand. Violet withdrew hers gently and kept them out of reach from then on.

"I'm sorry, Alistair, but no. I've never felt more than a mild attraction for you." She hated to admit even that much. "But we can't base a relationship on that." Now she'd experienced greater depth with Nick, simple attraction was nowhere near enough.

"Of course. But think about what we could achieve together. We could make your daddy's company a household name. Can't you see it?" Alistair raised his hands as though he was visioning a billboard or a newspaper headline. "Harrington-Reynolds takes the tourism industry by storm."

Violet could not hold back her amusement. Harrington-Reynolds? He'd already planned their PR gimmicks? "And what is your vision for the company?" she asked, lips twitching.

"I've been working on projections. Together, I believe we can increase the profit of both our families' companies twofold."

Violet sipped at a glass of water. "What do you see my role as in this new conglomerate?" This felt more like a job interview than a date.

Alistair leaned toward her, eyes bright with enthusiasm. "You would continue in even more of a public role. Look at you.

The cameras love you. You could sell honey to a bee with that smile. Together, we can double that impact." He gave a light shrug. "I've been on a magazine cover or two myself."

Oh yes. She vaguely recalled he'd modelled for a couple of cologne ads back in his late teens. Now he graced the front of financial magazines. Still handsome. But a different product.

"What about starting a family? Where does that fit in?" Not that she had any intentions of agreeing to any of this, but she had promised Daddy to hear him out. And she was curious. Did he have any thoughts outside of his ambition?

Alistair's gaze dropped again. "It doesn't, really. But does that matter? I mean, most couples start having children later these days. We've got at least ten years before we need to think about a family."

Interesting. He didn't even ask what she thought. She dabbed at her mouth with the napkin, folded it and rose from the table. Drew followed suit.

"Alistair, you've given me a lot to consider. Do you mind giving me some time to digest it all?" Not that she needed to digest anything. She'd already made up her mind, but the time would be good for him to keep his distance.

He also stood and came around the table. "Sure Vi, I can do that." He leaned in to kiss her and she turned so that his lips landed on her cheek.

"I'll call you," she said as they parted. He probably wouldn't wait as long as she wanted him to, but for now, the pressure was off.

The pilot announced they were nearing the drop zone. Violet pushed all thoughts of Alistair—and Nick—aside. She needed to focus on the jump. If she passed this test, she'd have the license to do the formation dives she was aiming for. With a quick prayer and a check of their position, Violet called the jump and let herself fall from the plane along with the instructor and other divers. The instructor became the base they all aimed for and connected with. Then they all turned, changed position, and connected again. They repeated this once more before separating, deploying their chutes safely, then heading for the landing site.

———

NICK WAITED IMPATIENTLY OUTSIDE the debrief room. Was it possible to be more nervous than Violet about the outcome of her dive? Some people made several attempts at the license before they achieved it. And rightly so. After all, one wrong move in the sky could mean death. He tried to focus on packing the parachutes—another precision task Violet had seemed to learn effortlessly.

Finally, she emerged from the room, her gaze immediately seeking him. Her eyes were bright. Spotting him, she practically skipped over to him.

"You got it?" He dropped the chute he was working on.

"I got it." She ran into his open arms.

"Congratulations." He embraced her tightly, then gently moved her to arm's length. "You are amazing."

"Thank you." She nodded. "Now to finalize the air show. You know we only have two weeks to go?"

"Two weeks." Two weeks to see if Morgan Reynolds would soften towards him. Two weeks to know if he was to stay in America with Violet or fly home to Australia and his family. Nick blew out a long breath. "First, can we celebrate?"

"What do you have in mind?" Violet's face lit up even further, and his insides somersaulted again.

"I'd suggest a candlelit dinner for two, but that might not be a good idea right now." For more reasons than one.

"Agreed." Violet giggled.

"How about we go out somewhere simple, like Joe's Diner.

We could invite Tony, and Amelia, Bree, and your other girl-friends."

"That's a great idea." Violet tapped a finger on his chest. "But to make it all look fair and inclusive, we should probably invite Alistair as well. And Drew will likely tag along."

Nick gritted his teeth at Alistair's name, and Violet saw his hesitation.

"I know it's not ideal. And I have no intentions toward him. But with all the rumors flying around, if people see me with both of you at the same time, they won't know what to believe. Especially if I don't favor either of you with particular attention. It can just be a party of friends. Okay?"

Although he didn't like it, Nick could see her logic. That evening he watched her as she sat between Amelia and Breanna, barely looking at either him or Alistair. What was going on inside her head. Did she find this easy? He certainly didn't. The least he could do was pretend to ignore her as much as she did him, and hopefully throw people off, even if almost everyone at the table knew exactly how they felt about each other. They even played along. Perhaps Violet had clued them in beforehand.

Alistair scowled at him frequently, and Nick forced a smile in response. Alistair was forever leaving the table to take one phone call or another. Even at the table, he was often tapping messages out, despite the laughter and fun going on around him. Lilly, bless her, distracted Alistair whenever it appeared he would try to approach Violet, and he didn't press his point.

Thankfully, Nick had Tony beside him. They engaged in a long conversation, which kept his mind and attention occupied and away from his longing for Violet.

Finally, after they had all toasted Violet on her success, everyone drifted home. Taking the nudge from Tony, Nick followed him out the door after a quick goodbye wave to Violet.

He had barely walked in the door of the Bible College when his phone pinged with a message from Violet.

That was hard.

Understatement. Of. The. Year.

True. You okay?

Yes. It was a great night. But it would have been so much better if I were next to you, holding your hand.

Nick's heart throbbed.

One day soon, eh?

I hope so, Nick.

Me too.

But thank you for tonight.

Anything for you.

XXOO

Goodnight. XXOO

Nick held his phone to his chest and breathed out. How did four little characters suddenly mean so much?

In his room, he pulled open the bedside drawer and pulled out his air ticket. He'd booked for the twenty-eighth of August. Two and a half weeks away. It was a flexible ticket, so he could change the date if he wanted to, but this seemed like a deadline racing toward him. *Lord, please show me one way or the other before then.* This not knowing was killing him.

Nick smirked as he readied himself for bed. It would be typical of the Lord to leave the answer until the last minute. Hadn't he seen that already so many times in his life? It seemed God wanted to stretch and strengthen people's faith and patience as they waited for Him to come through.

All right, Lord. I'm waiting, and I'm trusting in you.

The following morning, as he ate a breakfast of cereal and toast, he opened his laptop to check his email. Messages from his family were always welcome, and he smiled at the updates from his sisters and parents. But amongst all the junk email, was an odd email from Wild Blue Yonder Tours, a scenic flight company based in Miami, Florida. Nick frowned as he opened the email.

Dear Mr. Gordon,

Your resume has come across our desk and we are pleased to offer you a position as a tour guide on our Miami Beach scenic flights.

Wait. What? How did his resume go anywhere? Nick certainly hadn't sent it. He read the letter of offer, which detailed a salary package that far exceeded what he earned now, and even what he had earned back in Darwin. It included a generous health insurance package and covered his relocation expenses to Miami.

If he were looking for a job, this would be amazing. The climate in Miami would be like summer all year around, but a little cooler than Darwin. And Miami was a well-known tourist destination. But who had put him forward for this job?

Something in the pit of his stomach niggled. This was a tourist company. He wondered …

A few clicks on the browser and he found the connection he suspected. Wild Blue Yonder Tours had an affiliation with The Reynolds Group. Morgan Reynolds was behind the offer. Another attempt to get him out of Violet's life with the lure of money. And Miami was about as far away from Washington State as he could get.

Nick shook his head. Did Mr. Reynolds think everyone centered their life on fortune?

"What's got you so bothered this morning?"

Nick looked up to see Pete Franklin standing there, hot coffee in hand.

"Morgan Reynolds is trying to buy me off again."

"Is that right?"

"Mm-hm. I feel insulted that he thinks I'm so shallow."

"Well, he doesn't actually know you, does he?"

"No. It would be nice if he gave me the time of day. But that's unlikely. He has decided who I am and what my motives are without asking me a single question."

"What are you going to do about it?" Pete sat down next to him.

"Not much I can do except decline the job offer."

"Job offer?"

"Yeah. Check this out." He turned his laptop so Pete could read the letter. "Reynolds owns the company, so he's clearly behind the offer. The salary package is way higher than it should be."

Pete let out a low whistle. "Does Violet know about this?"

"I highly doubt it. She'd be furious."

"Will you tell her?"

"Probably not. She doesn't need more reasons to fight with her father. I'll keep it cool for now unless I need to tell her. I'll turn down the offer and quietly stand my ground. I'm just praying the Lord will intervene on my behalf."

"You really love her, don't you?"

"More than I can say," Nick swallowed, his throat at once thick.

"Well, I'll pray for you, too."

CHAPTER EIGHTEEN

Almost two weeks had flown by in a mess of preparation and planning, practice and organization. Even though the Masters of the Sky Air Show was an annual event and most of it was planned months ago, the skydiving exhibit was a recent addition, and Violet scrambled with her event coordinator and team to get everything ready in time. Two weeks in Europe hadn't helped, and now they were under the pump.

Violet had little time to spare, trying to keep the balance between Nick, Alistair, and her father. At least including Alistair in some things had given her a clearer path to talk to Daddy. Poor Nick waited in the wings while she tried to sort it all out.

Not that she ignored Nick. Not at all. They talked every evening and sent each other frequent messages during the day. He watched from a distance as she worked with the professional formation divers who'd flown in, sending her a wink whenever he got the chance to make eye contact. Not for one instant did she doubt that she had his full support. But she longed for the day she could openly stand side by side with him.

The closer it came to the day of the Air Show, the more Daddy seemed to relax. She figured he believed Nick would soon fly home to Australia—no doubt he'd found a way to learn Nick's booking details. Violet already knew Nick had a ticket, but could change it if he wanted to, so she wasn't worried. It was just a matter of whether her father would change his attitude.

Violet challenged Daddy one evening. "Like I said the other day, I'm not sure I'm cut out for a high-flying business role."

"Of course you are. You were born for this. That Nick Gordon fellow has just put silly ideas in your head. That's all."

"And we're back to that again." Violet groaned. "Did Mom tell you about our talk?"

A pause on the line. "Yes." He dragged the word out, obviously, not wanting to admit the fact.

"Even she thinks I don't fit in the business world." Would he take note of what Mom thought?

"She shouldn't have said those things." He sounded gruff. "We only did what was best for you. And look at the amazing young woman you've turned out to be."

Violet chewed her lip. What was she supposed to say to that? "You really think so?"

"Of course I do. I've always been proud of you and your accomplishments. Just don't throw it all away on an emotional whim."

"Emotional whim—?" Once again, it was the implication that she should ignore her emotions. Violet clenched her teeth as anger surged.

"Give yourself time. You'll get over this infatuation and come to your senses."

"Infatuation?" He still didn't trust her with decisions. Still thought she was a flighty flibbertigibbet. Still thought she was impulsive and irrational. After all these years. Violet swallowed down the angry retort that came to her lips and released a heavy sigh instead. "I am giving it time. I've spent more time with Alistair, as you asked. Will you please give me a little credit?"

A breath. Two. "At least you're taking this seriously at last."

Violet could only shake her head, refusing to be baited. "Very seriously." He was still too rigid. He wouldn't listen if she tried to tell him about the wonderful man Nick was. Despite seeming more relaxed, his heels remained planted deep in the ground of his wishes. Time to change the subject. "Are you coming to the air show?"

"Of course I am, Vi. I wouldn't miss it for the world. Your mom and I will fly in the night before. Can you make sure the housekeeper has our room ready?"

"I'll have her put fresh linen on the bed and everything else you need."

"Good. Thanks, sweet pea. I'll see you soon."

Violet sat with her head in her hands for several minutes. How was she going to get through to him? *Please, Lord, show me the way.*

Now the day of the event was looming. She and Amelia sat at their desks going through lists of tasks.

"Do you have your speech ready?" Amelia asked.

"Yes. I drafted it and sent to Haven of Hope to check."

"And they are sending someone to share their story?"

"Correct."

Amelia ticked a couple of boxes on her notepad. "You have all your jump gear ready to go?"

"Check. Already in the trunk."

"Good. I was on the phone with the event coordinators earlier. They confirmed the sausage sizzle and hotdog stands are all organized. Volunteers from the church will man them. All the tech is arranged for the livestream, and there will be tech support on the ground should any hiccups arise."

"What about the LED screen?" Violet asked.

"Is being set up today, along with the staging, and AV equipment."

"Great. And we have the capacity for donations for Haven of Hope?"

"Yeah. When the screen isn't being used for the live stream of your dive, it will show video promotions for them, including success stories from several women, and online options for donating. There'll be several donation tins for cash, at the food stalls and info desk. And there's a tap-and-go credit card giving station."

Violet released a long breath. "It sounds like everything is good to go. Now we just hope the weather holds out."

"I've been watching the forecast for a couple of weeks. It's promising to be a good day."

Violet shook her hands, nerves suddenly hitting. "But you never know. Forecasts aren't always accurate." This was becoming very real.

"Freefall Adventures are flying in a second Cessna Caravan so they can run several celebrity tandem jumps."

"And they're all going to be livestreamed too, yes?"

"Absolutely. We've advertised all the people who are jumping, so we should get a good crowd. More than those who are just interested in planes and cars, anyway. I mean, we've covered a lot—we have sports stars, film stars, blogging celebrities, online influencers, and even a couple of well-known locals. It's a wide variety."

Violet's heart rate increased. This was going to be so good. Hopefully, they could all pull it off. "What about music?"

"I believe Nick had a word to the band leader at Trinity Lakes Community Church, and they'll do a few sets of cover songs for us. Apparently, they're quite good. When they're not playing, we'll stream some background music."

Tears sprang to Violet's eyes, overwhelmed by the way people were jumping in to help with this cause. "I'm so proud of this event, Amelia." She tugged a tissue from a nearby box and dabbed at her eyes. "I know it started as a way for you guys to build my confidence, but it's so much more than that now."

Perhaps she'd found her purpose, to raise awareness for some of the desperate needs in the world. Make an impact. With the contacts she'd built over the years, she had access to companies who would donate time, expertise, goods, and services to help her raise significant funds. This, was worth pursuing. *Lord, is this what you created me to do?*

"And I am proud to be by your side. I know you. You would never have let this be about you, even though we tried. It's amazing what we've been able to pull together, isn't it?" Amelia pushed her chair back and came over, wrapping her in a warm hug. "I am so glad to work for and with my best friend."

Violet squeezed her in return. "Me too, Amelia." She pulled back and wiped at her tears again. "You know that means you can never quit, right?"

Amelia laughed. "As if."

Violet joined her in laughter, although she knew their paths would probably separate one day. It was unrealistic to think otherwise. But for now, this was a perfect partnership.

"Right. Well, I'm going to go over my script once more. Then I'm going to study my formation dive plans until I know them back to front."

Amelia rolled her eyes. "You already know them back to front."

"Well, front to back then." Violet grinned.

Amelia glanced at her smartwatch. "Just don't forget your parents are arriving in a couple hours. Are you meeting them at the airport?"

"Drew will collect them and bring them back here. But yes, I need to prepare myself for that, too."

———

Four days.

Four days until the flight left for Australia, either with him or without him. Nick rubbed his hands across his face. He still had no idea where things stood. Correction. He knew exactly where they stood—not where he wanted them to stand. According to Violet, her father hadn't budged an inch. Nick groaned. *Lord, help me.*

He'd vowed to keep things platonic between himself and Violet until her daddy gave his approval, but now that they were coming so close to the decision date, he didn't know how he'd tear himself away. Oh, how he loved her. And she loved him, too. They both knew they were meant to be together. What would be so wrong with running away with her and being happy? The urge to take matters into his own hands was stronger than ever. *Please, Jesus?*

Thankfully, he'd organized a video call with his family tonight, lunchtime on Saturday for them. Surely they would help his desperate and scrambling thoughts to settle. He needed to pull it together, at least for tomorrow, for the air show. It was going to be a monumental day.

Nick drew a deep breath as he made the call. The picture of his family appeared on the second ring, and there they were. All of them. Smiling, teasing, filling his heart like nothing else could. He listened as they all filled him in on the news from home. Uncle Willy was much better now, although having to make some lifestyle changes. Shelly was cramming, getting ready for her NTCET—high school certificate. Exams were due to begin in less than two months, and she was determined to get a good ATAR score in order to go to university.

Cathy and Isaac popped into the middle of the screen, Isaac's arms around Cathy's waist, the two of them glowing. An ache developed deep in Nick's chest. He was happy for them, really. He just yearned for the same with Violet.

"Do you think you'll be back for the wedding, Nick?" his sister asked.

Nick groaned internally. "More than likely, it seems." He dropped his head into his hands. He didn't want them to see the disappointment on his face. Didn't want them to think he wasn't excited to be there.

"Oh, Nicky." Mum's voice. Full of compassion.

When Nick looked up, the rest of the family was gone, and only she and Dad remained.

"Not going so well, eh, son?" Dad asked.

Nick could only shake his head, a lump developing in his throat.

"I'm so sorry to hear that." Mum's eyes were wide with sincerity. "I can see how much she means to you."

"What are you going to do?" Dad's face was a mask of seriousness.

"What I want to do … what I want …" Visions of sweeping Violet into his arms flashed through his mind. Visions of jumping into his car with her and driving a thousand kilometers. Maybe to Vegas. Nick shook his head and groaned for the hundredth time that day.

Not my will, but Yours be done.

A verse from the gospels dropped into his head, from Jesus praying in the Garden of Gethsemane, about to face death on a cross. He prayed for a way out, yet, in the end, He laid down what He wanted to follow God's path.

"I have to let it go." He choked the words out.

Dad nodded and Mum pressed a hand to her mouth, tears welling in her eyes. "You have to let it go."

In that moment, peace flooded him again as his parents prayed for him. They prayed for strength and comfort and wisdom—everything he needed.

Barely seconds after he ended the call with his parents, his phone rang.

Violet.

"Hey." She sounded miserable, and his heart melted all over again.

"What's up? Are you okay?"

"Daddy's here." A long pause. Those two words and the tone she used told him much. "He's never going to change, Nick." Her voice broke.

Nick gritted his teeth. It was hard to hear, though he already knew it, and he wanted to reassure her. "Maybe he needs more time." That sounded pathetic.

"I don't care anymore." A hard edge came into her voice. "I'm coming to Australia with you."

Nick's heart pelted stones at his head as wisdom fought with yearning. Oh, how he would love that.

Not my will, but Yours be done.

Ugh. Precious. There was no way he could fight the Lord. "You can't, Violet." His voice was thick.

"Of course I can. We can put all this mess behind us and just be together. It's not like it's never been done before. We can make it work. Can't you see it?"

The plea in her voice was unmistakable. Every fiber of his being wanted to reach out and hold her, comfort her, say yes to her. He stood and paced the room, willing his heart to stop breaking as he pushed out the words he knew he must say.

"We have to let it go."

Silence for a beat. Two. "What do you mean?"

Nick sucked in his breath and released it, shaking. "I mean fully surrender. As much as I love you—and I do, you know that, right?"

"Yes." She sounded wary now. "And I love you, too. But …?"

"I feel the Lord is telling us to lay it all down. Let it go."

"What?" Her breath came quickly. "Nick, are you telling me it's over? Are you breaking up with me before we even got together?"

Pain shot through him like a knife slicing butter. "No!" He hated the sound of that. Rejected it, even. But, oh, he couldn't deny it either. If God was asking him to lay it down, there was no guarantee He would ever give it back. "I guess. Maybe. I suppose I am. I'm so sorry Violet."

The line went dead as she hung up on him. Nick crumpled to the floor on his knees, heart crying out to the God who seemed so unfair in this moment. Yet, deep down, peace reigned and Nick knew his decision was right, despite the raging emotions that threatened to drown him. *Lord, help me get through tomorrow.*

It would be easy to pull out of the event. Easy on his emotions, perhaps. But he would regret it. Feel like a deserter. Somehow, he must soldier on for another twenty-four hours. Perhaps he could bring his flight forward after that. Tomorrow was going to be his last day with Freefall Adventures anyway. Without that job and without Violet, there was nothing to hold him here.

Despite the fact that he needed it, sleep eluded him. Nick tossed and turned for hours, heart rent over the loss of his hopes and dreams. It didn't matter that it was the right thing to do, he would still grieve. He was going to miss Violet like the air he breathed.

Just after two a.m. his phone screen lit up. Although it was on silent, it still responded to a message coming through. Sometimes friends and family in Australia messaged him in their daytime, even though it was the middle of the night in Trinity Lakes. Since he was awake, he picked it up and tried to focus. He jerked into a sitting position when he saw the text was from Violet.

Sorry for hanging up on you. I know you're right. I prayed and felt that Jesus was saying the same thing to me. So, as hard as it is, I will not bear any hard feelings toward you. But please don't leave tomorrow without saying goodbye.

Strangely, her message sent relief flowing through him. He put his phone back on his charger and lay back. Seconds later, he picked it up again and sent her a string of emoticons, including flooding tears and a broken heart.

Finally, Nick slept, although it only seemed like minutes before his alarm went off. He needed to be at the airfield by seven. He shoved some breakfast down his throat while he packed water, a change of clothes, snacks, sunscreen, and whatever else he might need into his backpack. Who knew when he'd get to eat again? Yet he'd need the energy, so he grabbed a banana to eat on the road.

His stomach churned at the thought of seeing Violet. Would there be awkwardness, stiffness, between them? Perhaps their paths wouldn't cross many times during the day. After all, she was going to be flat-out between speaking, skydiving, and campaigning for Haven of Hope with the crowd.

Yet when he entered the hangar, there she was, in all her jaw-dropping brilliance, offering him a shy smile. Nick tried to shove his emotions back down like he'd shove a pillow into its cover.

"Morning." The only word he could find.

"Morning." She seemed to have the same difficulty.

"All set?" He raised his brows at her.

"Yes. I think so." She breathed out.

"You'll be great." He wanted to reach out and squeeze her arm, but he kept his hands busy fiddling with his backpack.

"Thanks. I hope so."

Yeah, okay. This was going to get awkward real quick. "I'd better go and ..." He gestured toward the parachutes hanging along the wall. "You know."

"Sure. See you later?" Violet's eyes said it all. *Don't forget your promise to say goodbye.*

Nick could only nod and sidle past her to prepare for the day.

CHAPTER NINETEEN

Violet watched Nick's retreating form, thankful their meeting hadn't been too difficult. No, the hard part would come later, saying goodbye forever. She closed her eyes and tried to put those thoughts aside. For the next several hours, she needed to focus on the cause. Trafficked women had far worse problems to deal with than her, and she owed it to them to give them her best.

She found Amelia going over the run sheet again. The time slot for the skydiving segment was from two to three o'clock in the afternoon. In that time, there would be two groups of tandem dives, one formation dive with the professionals, then her livestreamed formation dive. The weather was perfect. Sunshine, a cloudless sky and a light, fresh breeze. *Thank you, Jesus.*

The speeches would run from two-thirty, and the music before that, in gaps between dives and at the end. Before that, there would be displays from old war planes, aerobatics displays, fighter jet displays. On the ground, kids and families could climb inside old planes and learn the history.

During that early part of the show, Frank Martinez and his

team would promote Freefall Adventures, while she worked with Haven of Hope to raise awareness of trafficking and gain donations for the organization. That would mean she and Nick would be separated for most of the day … which felt like a good thing and a bad thing at the same time.

Several times she sought him out—not to talk to him or anything, just to see what he was up to—and either saw him showing young kids the parachutes and how the canopies worked or showing videos of skydiving examples. Then, when sadness threatened to overtake her, she walked away again. Back to her own mingling with the crowd.

Daddy, Mom, Alistair, and Drew turned up at lunchtime and kept her busy while she made sure they found food and drinks. The Australian contingent from church—the Laden family— was waving everyone over to their barbecue where they cheerfully sold sausages in bread, engaging in lighthearted competition with the hot dog stand.

"I haven't tried these yet." Violet turned to her parents. "You want to have some with me?"

"Sure. I'm willing to try." Mom said.

Alistair wrinkled his nose. "I think I'll find something else." He headed off toward the main exhibition building.

Daddy was silent but took two sausages. He nodded after taking his first bite. "Not bad. I like the onions."

Violet bit into hers. "The onion is definitely good."

Checking the time, she finished her sausage quickly and washed it down with a soda. "I need to get going. We are doing the presentation in a few minutes."

"So I should get my check book ready?" Daddy winked at her.

"Absolutely." Violet grinned. At least he was behind her with this. Her heart panged again. If only he'd got on board with Nick.

"Break a leg, sweet pea."

"It's not that kind of stage, Daddy." She giggled. "But thanks." She glanced around her. "Tell Alistair whenever he gets back."

"Will do."

Violet found Amelia, who handed her the cue cards for her speech. "Thanks Amelia."

"Are you nervous?"

"A little. But it's not like I haven't done public speaking before."

Amelia put a finger to her ear. She was connected via radio to the event coordinators. She listened momentarily and then nodded to Violet. "You're up."

Violet took a deep breath and ascended the stairs to the stage. Applause met her as the emcee introduced her. "Thank you and welcome to Freefall for Freedom," she said once behind the microphone. Violet presented information and statistics on the trafficking industry, highlighting the soul-destroying effects it had on the victims. She welcomed the crowd to join her in supporting their efforts to fight this trade and free women from its clutches.

"We have a special guest here today who is incredibly brave and would like to share her story with you." Violet stretched her hand out to the side of the stage. "Welcome, Serena."

"Serena" approached the microphone and related her terrible tale. Violet didn't know the woman's real name, and she wore sunglasses and a wig to hide her identity. She was still in danger from those who had sold her in the first place. Serena was courageous, and Violet only hoped she could be that strong when life turned against her.

While the young woman talked, Violet scanned the crowd, who were all captivated and appalled by what they were hearing. She could see Nick at the back, leaning against a wall, ankles crossed and arms folded, but hanging on every word. And Alistair was … right over there, with his phone to his ear. Of course. Violet pressed her lips together and continued to gaze over the audience. There were her parents, also listening carefully, holding hands. Another pang. If only …

She shook herself free of her nostalgia as Serena finished her story by thanking the selfless workers who rescued her.

The crowd clapped as Violet returned to the mic and Serena left the stage. "Thank you to Serena and thank you to those who, at risk of their own safety, dare to go into those situations and save those girls." The people continued to clap.

"Now, please turn your attention to the screen behind me as we hear from more women who have been freed. While they share their stories, we will prepare the first of today's dives. The first will be tandem jumps with Mitchell Reilly, our local ice-hockey hero." She paused as a cheer went up. "Adam Lancaster, physio and blogger extraordinaire." Another roar. The crowd's reactions made this even more fun than she expected. "And social influencer Heidi Klassen." Violet named the rest of the celebrities with similar responses, then relinquished the stage to the emcee.

Amelia met her at the bottom of the steps. "Perfect. That was so good."

Daddy pushed through the closest people then. "I agree. You had them eating out of your hand, Vi."

Mom gave her a hug. "I'm so proud of you."

"I'm not done yet." Violet laughed. "I still have to jump myself." She glanced at her watch. "Which reminds me, I need to get over there and get suited up. I'm due to take off in half an hour."

On her way to the hangar, she spotted Tony, who approached her with a hug and a kiss on the cheek. "You're doing great today, Violet."

"Thanks, Tony. So good to see you here."

"Where else would I be?"

Violet giggled. "I appreciate it."

A brief conversation later, she parted from him and jogged

to the hangar, ready to change into her jumpsuit and get her parachute on. Nick soon drifted in, returning from the first tandem dive with Mitch Reilly, parachute in tow. The two of them laughed together like old friends.

Violet checked and rechecked her straps and equipment along with the formation divers around her, only to discover Nick right beside her.

"People are loving the livestream of the tandems," he told her.

"That's good."

"They're all getting to see what I see on almost a daily basis."

"What's that?"

"The first expressions of someone as they fall out of a plane for the first time." He grinned. "It never gets old."

"Oh yeah? Do you remember mine?"

"If I remember correctly, you screamed."

Violet laughed. "It was a good scream." Heat flooded her face as she remembered being strapped to him so close, in the plane, in the fall, landing on the ground. All those jumps they'd made together over the last few months flashed through her memory. Was it really all over? Just like that. If only she'd trusted him from day one, taken responsibility for her own mistake, perhaps Daddy would never have doubted him either. It was too late for those what ifs, though. He was leaving in a few days.

"Yeah, it was a good scream." He broke into her runaway thoughts.

She had to get away from him before her heart caved in again. "Well, I'd better get on the plane."

"Sure. You'll be great." He stepped aside a little.

"Thanks."

Nick raised his fist in the air. "Blue skies."

Violet tapped her fist against his. "Blue skies."

She drew in several deep breaths as she walked away from

him. Strange how leaving Nick's side seemed harder than jumping out of a plane.

"You ready for this?" One of the formation divers caught her attention.

"As ready as I can be." Violet forced a smile.

They all climbed into the sky caravan and waited as the plane took off down the runway, thrust upwards, rising higher and higher and circling back around to the drop zone. Two jumpers who would operate as cameramen sat nearby, cameras mounted on their helmets. They both switched their equipment on, and Violet looked into the lens.

"Hi, everybody." She waved, grinning. "We're just approaching the drop zone now."

The door opened, and they all moved close, the two cameramen swinging outside and hanging on to the edges. When Violet received the okay, she yelled, "Freefall for Freedom," and they all tumbled out of the plane.

NICK FIXED his eyes on the screen. He'd stopped packing the parachutes to run and watch Violet's dive. A smooth exit. Seconds later, they formed into a star. The divers continued to turn and re-grip, completing two more formations. All the while, the divers with the cameras stayed close, giving everyone a fantastic view of what the group was doing.

Violet's hot pink dive suit stood out from all the others in black and gray, so she was easy to watch. Thirty-odd seconds later, they all broke apart into separate directions. The crowd roared and cheered with their success.

Amid the excitement, Nick noticed something that made his heart catapult. Violet had released her canopy, but the lines seemed to be tangled and her canopy didn't fully open. And she was dropping out of view of the camera, as the cameraman had deployed his canopy perfectly.

Nick's breath caught. *Jesus, help her.*

The crowd gasped in horror as Violet continued to fall faster than any of the others. Five seconds ticked by like an eternity as Nick continued to pray. He'd never felt so useless in his life. There was nothing he could do.

C'mon, Violet. You know what to do.

A couple screams rose around him. He was sure one was Violet's mother. Who would want to watch their daughter spiral like that? Nick glanced sideways to see Mrs. Reynolds burying her face against her husband's chest. And Morgan Reynolds's face was ashen. But his eyes met Nick's with an unmistakable appeal.

Dear Lord, he will blame me for this.

Everything in those seconds moved in slow motion. Every detail of every terrified face around him. Every cry of anguish. But Nick knew there was hope. Violet was well-trained. He lifted his gaze back to the sky.

Emergency procedures, Vi. Do it now.

And finally, the tangled chute detached, and her backup canopy deployed. And finally, Nick breathed again. But then, every sense was alert, ready for action. He bolted toward the ATV that stood ready if needed. Violet would miss the landing target, coming in as fast as she was. He needed to get to her right now.

As he jumped into the vehicle, Morgan Reynolds raced up behind him.

"Quick. Get in."

Mr. Reynolds looked over his shoulder. Who was he looking for? His wife? Alistair?

"I'm not waiting," Nick said stiffly. His earpiece told him all runway activity was halted until Violet was cleared.

Mr. Reynolds nodded briefly and climbed in. He was barely seated before Nick took off as fast as the ATV would go.

"Is she … will she be all right?" Mr. Reynolds stammered, his face still pale.

"I'm sure she'll be fine. She is a very competent diver, sir." Nick could still see her in the air ahead. He prayed she wouldn't injure herself on the ground. Prayed his assurances to her father would hold. Violet knew how to land. He had to trust in her abilities. And in God.

There. She landed just in front of a bank of trees. Slid. Rolled. Stayed, unmoving, as the canopy collapsed to the ground around her. Nick pulled up the ATV, practically fell out of the driver's seat, and stumbled till he gained his footing. He raced to her side, Mr. Reynolds close on his heels.

"Violet!" they both called as they ran.

Nick dropped to his knees beside her. "Violet, are you okay?"

Her body shook as she cried. "I'm okay. I'm alive."

"Can you move?" Mr. Reynolds kneeled on the other side of her.

"Yes. I think so. I'm just enjoying the earth beneath me." She let out a half-laugh.

"So, no pain?" Nick had to double-check.

"No. I'm fine. Just shaken." As evidence, she sat up and her father assisted her to stand, wrapping her in a bear-like embrace.

Nick glanced over his shoulder to see an ambulance approaching. "The medics are going to want to check you over."

"Thanks, Nick." She pulled away from her father and stepped into his arms, shaking and crying again. "I couldn't untangle it. I was so scared."

How could he not hold her after that terrifying ordeal? "I'm so glad you're okay. You did all the right things," he murmured against her hair.

Violet pulled back from him again and wiped at her eyes. "Well, I had an excellent teacher."

Mr. Reynolds took her by the arm and led her to the ambulance while Nick collected her parachute and took it to the ATV, his own body trembling now. How close had he come to losing her altogether? It was one thing for him to be separated from her on this earth, but she had so much to offer, even if he couldn't be by her side.

———

VIOLET SAT on the back of the ambulance, allowing the medics to examine her, while her father hovered about, fussing over her.

"Make sure she doesn't have a concussion," Mr. Reynolds ordered, as if they didn't know what they were doing.

"Did you lose consciousness at all, ma'am?" one paramedic obediently asked.

"No. Not at all."

They shone lights in her eyes. Asked her questions about the date, about where she was. All of which she answered confidently. The only thing wrong was this wretched shaking. Shock, they told her. And it would pass.

After a thorough examination, checking for broken bones and whatnot, the paramedics agreed she was fine to be released, on the proviso that if she suddenly became sleepy or dizzy, to go to emergency immediately.

"You may find that once the shock wears off, you'll feel all the bruises you don't feel now. Adrenaline has a way of masking injuries." The paramedic's gaze swerved to Daddy. "Keep an eye on her."

"You bet." He nodded. "Home to bed with you, sweet pea."

Violet straightened. "No. I'm fine."

"You heard the doctor."

"I did. But all my friends—and the rest of the crowd over there—are wondering what's happened to me. I need to get on that stage and reassure them."

And see Nick to say the last goodbye they'd promised each other. Where had he got to? She leaned sideways. He leaned against the ATV, waiting. "I'll go back with Nick."

"No." Daddy frowned at her. "I'll go back with Mr. Gordon. You can ride in the ambulance."

Her stomach clenched. He was still keeping them apart, even to the last. But right now, she didn't have the energy to fight. She shivered, and the paramedic wrapped a blanket around her shoulders.

"Yes, you should ride back with us," the paramedic said.

Violet sighed, complying with their wishes, though every part of her wanted to be with Nick. And yet, it seemed it couldn't be. She climbed into the ambulance and watched Nick until the doors closed him off from her sight. The next time she saw him would probably be the last. She closed her eyes as a tear slid down her cheek.

I was with you in the fall.

Violet's eyes shot open. Yes. In the sky, at that moment, although she was scared, she had been calm. Able to think through her training and what she needed to do to land safely. The steady presence of the Lord had been with her in every microsecond between the lines tangling and the emergency chute opening. It was only after she landed that the shaking and crying began.

And that was His promise to her now. That He would be with her in this fall. The breakup with Nick that now seemed inevitable. The Lord would walk with her through water, through fire, through any hardship. He promised to make beauty from pain and goodness from trouble. *Thank you, Jesus.* Her heart stilled. Indeed, her whole body stilled as His peace flooded her.

When the ambulance pulled up near the hangar, Violet stepped out onto the tarmac, unaided, and made her way toward the stage. People immediately rushed her and several security guards, including Drew and Tony, stepped in to help her—Tony giving her a wink and an affectionate squeeze of the arm.

Amelia, Breanna, and Lilly all surrounded her, arms in a tangle, weeping over her. "I'm fine girls. I'm fine." Violet giggled, trying to extricate herself.

"We were so worried about you." Amelia hiccupped. Violet suspected she'd been crying since it happened.

"Thank you. But part of the training was how to land safely in emergency situations." She tried to assure them.

"Do you think you will ever go up again?" Bree asked.

Violet laughed. "I don't think you could stop me." Although it might be less fun without Nick around.

Alistair broke through the circle then and wrapped her up tight. "I thought I'd lost you."

CHAPTER TWENTY

Nick watched Alistair possessively claiming Violet and leading her to the stage, arm in arm, with not a little envy. How he wished things had been different. But he had to get a grip. Morgan Reynolds had chosen Alistair for his daughter. End of story. That fact had come through pretty clearly on the ride back.

"You didn't take the job in Miami." A simple statement.

"No, sir." Nick had clenched his teeth. Mr. Reynolds had practically admitted organizing it with that comment.

"Why not?"

Nick swallowed. "If I'm not here with …" he couldn't say her name, it stuck in his throat with a choking sound. "If I'm not here in Trinity Lakes, I'm home in Australia with my family."

"And when are you flying back?"

As if he didn't already know the answer. "Tuesday. Earlier if I can get a flight."

"So you're no longer pursuing my daughter?"

Nick gripped the handlebars until his knuckles went white. Everything within him wanted to argue and fight for her, but he knew he couldn't. "No, sir." His voice wavered. "Not without your permission or approval."

Mr. Reynolds was silent. He probably thought Nick was weak. Not prepared to stand up for himself. So opposite to the men he was usually around, those cutthroat businessmen who would trample over anyone to get what they wanted.

Nick parked the ATV near the hangar, and Mr. Reynolds stepped down. He straightened his jacket and nodded to Nick.

"One thing, Mr. Reynolds." Nick couldn't help himself as the man turned away.

The stern man turned back to him with an eyebrow raised.

"I love her." Nick's voice shook with the strength of it. "I wanted you to know that."

Mr. Reynolds stared at him momentarily, then nodded slowly before walking away.

And now Nick watched Violet mount the steps to the stage to explain what had happened. A few minutes later, Amelia stepped up beside her and handed her a piece of paper. Violet opened the note and her eyes lit up.

"I have been informed that we have raised over one hundred thousand dollars for Haven of Hope today."

A cheer went up from the crowd, and Violet continued to thank everyone involved, naming several people. Nick lost track of what she was saying when Mr. Reynolds suddenly stepped up beside him again.

"May I have a word, Nick?"

"Sure." Nick shrugged. What the man wanted with him now, he had no idea.

Morgan Reynolds led him back away from the noisy crowd a little.

"What can I do for you, sir?"

Mr. Reynolds rubbed his hands together, looking thoughtful.

"I neglected to thank you for hurrying to assist Violet earlier. That was … inconsiderate of me."

Nick shook his head and scuffed his boots on the ground. "Anyone would have done the same."

"Yet, they didn't." Mr. Reynolds thrust his shoulders back and his chest out. "I've been speaking to my wife. Alistair didn't even see what happened. He wasn't watching at all. Too busy on a phone call."

Nick opened and closed his mouth. What was the man trying to say? "I'm not in a position to judge what he did or didn't do." Although Violet deserved better than that. Way better.

"You are far more gracious than I, Mr. Gordon."

What was he supposed to say to that? "Thank you. I think."

Mr. Reynolds shoved his hands in his pockets and rocked back and forth on his heels, silent for a moment. "Is it true that you have never … er … taken advantage of Violet in any way?"

Nick swiveled to look at him dead on, frowning in consternation.

"Tony tells me you were nothing but a gentleman with my daughter."

"I—"

"He also tried to tell me you were good for her."

What was happening? "That's very k—"

"To my shame, I fired him for giving his opinion."

"Oh." Nick's head was spinning. Why was Mr. Reynolds telling him all this? Confessing?

"My wife has also pointed out to me, several times now, that perhaps I have been behaving like a helicopter parent."

Nick coughed to smother an astonished laugh. Should he agree?

"I see you concur." He frowned.

"I didn't mean …"

Mr. Reynolds sighed. "The truth is, Nick … may I call you Nick?"

Nick nodded. What else was he going to do? Seriously, he must look like a stunned mullet.

"The truth is, until today, I have been blind to what is right in front of me. I don't want my daughter to be in a relationship with someone who is more interested in his business than in her or her wellbeing."

Okay, but where was this leading? "I thought you wanted a merger with Harrington and Sons."

Mr. Reynolds waved a hand dismissively. "A merger can happen either way. I thought he might make Violet happy. But it seems I've been so caught up in my plans for her that I lost sight of who she really is. Both she and Margaret have shown me that, too. And I haven't listened." A choked sob erupted. "I refused to listen, and now I've alienated myself from her." He straightened his shoulders and seemed to suck back his emotions again.

"You know she is my pride and my delight, don't you?"

"Of course she is, sir." This was all a bit overwhelming. A man-to-man, deep and meaningful conversation with someone, who minutes ago was antagonistic, to say the least. Precious.

"Morgan. Please call me Morgan."

Another surprise. "Okay. Morgan."

"Tell me one thing, Nick."

"Anything." Well, hopefully, nothing too serious.

"Does Violet hate me now?"

Nick blew out a relieved breath. "No, sir … Morgan. She is one hundred percent daddy's girl."

"Really?" Morgan's voice wavered again. Wonder of wonders. The great Morgan Reynolds had vulnerability, after all.

"Really." Nick nodded with a grin. "She may have been angry with you recently, and frustrated by your helicopter parenting, as you say. But above all, she just wants things to go back to normal between you."

"She does?"

Nick nodded, then dropped his gaze. "That's why we both decided we had to let the idea of a relationship between us go." Those words still hurt, no matter how many times he repeated them to himself.

"Both? You … talked about this?" Morgan seemed surprised.

Nick shrugged. There was no sense in holding anything back now. "Many times. Your opinion matters so much to her. There's no way she'd ever be happy without your support. She just wants you to believe in her, to trust her, to love her no matter what. And the last thing I wanted was to come between the two of you."

Morgan blinked rapidly. "Have I pushed her too far? Do you think she'll give me a chance to redeem myself?"

Nick's mouth curved into a grim smile. "I'm sure she will. But you should ask her yourself."

Morgan pulled out a handkerchief and blew his nose. "Yes. You're right. I've been wrong, and I need to make sure she knows that. I will talk to her."

"That's great, sir … er … Morgan. I'm happy for you both." He put out a hand for Morgan to shake. At least they would part as kind-of friends.

The man shook hands with him firmly. "Before I go, may I ask you one more thing?"

"Sure." What now?

"Do you think rather than bring your flight forward, you could shift it back a week? Or two?"

"Excuse me?" Now he was confused.

Mrs. Reynolds stepped up beside her husband then and slid her hand into his. "My wife and I would like to get to know you a little better, Nick." He turned to his wife. "Wouldn't we, love?"

"Yes." The woman, a clear image of her daughter, held out a hand. "It's nice to finally meet you. But a few words will not be enough, I'm afraid."

"Enough for what?" Nick's brows drew together again, his heart beginning to pound. "I'm sorry. What are you saying?"

"What do you think we're saying?" Morgan raised his brows, remaining elusive.

"Are you saying I can ..." Nick swallowed as his heart raced. "... date Violet?"

Morgan's face broke into a wide grin then, and he laughed. "Date her. Love her. Marry her. You have my—our blessing."

Nick stared at them dumbfounded, although his heart had taken flight. "What? I don't ... what made you change your mind?"

Morgan sighed. "I saw today what I should have seen all along. You love my girl. And more than that, you honor her. I have never met someone who stood firm for what he believes in, yet remained respectful at the same time. It would be foolish of me to ignore that. I can't imagine anyone better for her."

Nick still gawked at the man, his jaw slack. A wide-open door stood before him. One that had been locked tight for months. And now it seemed the world rushed in.

"Why are you still standing here, Nick?" Mrs. Reynolds asked. "Go to her."

———

VIOLET PACED UP and down inside the hangar. It was bad enough that Alistair had manhandled her as if he owned her. Then she'd seen Daddy upbraiding Nick. Oh yes, she'd seen the dumbfounded, shocked look on Nick's face. The way he shook his head. Daddy had gone too far. Both of them had gone too far. And now she'd be apologizing on their behalf again, instead of just enjoying a last talk with Nick before she had to say goodbye forever.

She waited impatiently. This was where he'd come, eventually. All the pack-up was starting, but weariness was creeping in.

It had been a long day and the shock of her skydiving incident was wearing off, leaving her exhausted. But she really needed to see Nick. Oh, where was he?

Finally, he slipped inside the hanger, and in seconds his gaze landed on her. His smile softened as he stopped and stared at her.

"You're a sight for sore eyes, you know that?" He greeted her.

Violet frowned. "What did Daddy say to you this time?" She wasn't about to be put off by him, pretending everything was fine.

Nick glanced around them, where several people milled about, packing down. "Not here." He took her by the hand and led her out behind the hangar. He leaned up against the corrugated iron wall and crossed his ankles, still looking like nothing bothered him. But she knew it wasn't true. Couldn't be true.

"Right. Well, what is it?" She leaned against the hangar beside him.

Nick cleared his throat and dropped his gaze to his boots. "He asked me to change my flight."

"I knew it." Violet growled. Actually growled. "Why does he still need to interfere when you're leaving?" Angry tears sprang to her eyes, and she pressed her hands to her face. "Saying goodbye was already going to be hard enough."

He swooped around in front of her. "Oh Vi, I'm sorry. I didn't mean to upset you." He stroked her hair, brushing his thumb beneath her eyes to wipe away the tears. "He actually asked me to shift it further away—like mid-September."

"What? Why?" Her tears stopped abruptly, confusion taking over.

Nick slipped one arm around her waist, then the other. "Because. Well. Because he's seen the error of his ways and is now happy for us to be together." He smiled into her eyes, his own glowing with tenderness.

Violet's heart stalled, then took wing. "What? Did I hear you correctly?"

Nick's eyes drifted to her lips. "Your Daddy wants me to date you, to love you, to—"

"Stop talking and kiss me already."

A gurgle of laughter bubbled up from deep in his chest. "Yes, ma'am."

But he still took his time, leaning in ever so slowly, brushing his nose against hers, planting a feathery kiss just above her top lip, before capturing her mouth gently with his. And oh, her heart soared as she curled her arms around his neck, and he deepened the kiss, reminding her of exactly why she had fallen for him.

Minutes must have ticked by before they parted a little, although he never removed his arms from around her. "By the way." She put her palms on his chest. "The answer is yes."

One eyebrow raised and Nick quirked his head to the side. "To what?"

"The question you asked me on the airplane that day—the second time we went up, I think."

A self-conscious laugh erupted. "You heard that, did you? I thought I might have to ask you again."

"Well, I won't complain if you do."

"But I already have your answer now." He murmured, eyes drifting to her lips again.

"Mm-hm." She couldn't keep the smug grin from her face.

"I love you Violet Reynolds." He kissed her.

"I love you, too, Nicky-Ned Flanders-Gordon." She kissed him back.

"Will." Another kiss. "You." And again. "Marry." A longer one this time. "Me?"

Violet pulled back from him, mischief rising. "Maybe." She backed away, flashing him an arch grin.

"Maybe?" Nick followed her.

"I have to see what Daddy says." She turned to run and laughed as he caught her and swiftly drew her back into his arms.

"Too late. He seems keen to have me for a son-in-law."

Violet stared at him wide-eyed. "Has he really come to his senses?"

"He has." Nick sobered. "He'll probably want to have a long chat with you."

Violet searched his gaze. He was completely serious. What a turnaround.

"Enough," his eyes shuttered. "Back to the subject at hand."

Violet couldn't keep the smile from her face. "What was that?"

"You were agreeing to marry me. Violet, I've known you were the one for me since the day I met you. I can't see my life without you. Please say you'll be mine?"

"Oh, I'm yours all right. Forever and always."

His face glowed as he gazed down at her. "Good. So that makes us extra, extra, special friends now, right?"

Violet laughed and pulled his head toward her and their lips met in a sizzling promise of forever.

———

Nick and Violet sat on the airplane, hands entwined, as the plane sped down the runway to take off. It had been two amazing weeks with her parents. Mr. and Mrs. Reynolds had stayed on in Trinity Lakes to spend time with Nick. And since he'd finished his contract with Freefall Adventures, he had a lot of time on his hands, unless he was working at the Bible College grounds or electrical maintenance at the church.

Daddy had sat down with her and spent hours apologizing for his behavior and asking her for forgiveness. It surprised her to find forgiveness came easily, especially knowing how much the Lord had forgiven her. And with Nick's encouragement and support to work through some of her emotions, they had begun to mend their damaged relationship.

Daddy even listened as she shared her heart with him about how she saw her future and her role with the Reynolds Group. Two days ago, he'd come to her with a proposal. How would she like to head up the charity arm of the company? She could run events like Freefall for Freedom and raise funds for worthy causes of her choosing.

"What do you think, Nick?" she'd asked him, knowing this would impact his future, too.

"I'm happy to support you in that," he'd said after they discussed it for a time. Nick would likely retrain for his electrical certificate so he could do contract work in the States. And still have time for the odd skydiving adventure.

Now, they were heading back to Australia so she could meet his family—although she had already met them online a few times. But face-to-face would be so much better. They'd arrive in time to attend his sister Cathy's wedding. Then Nick planned to tie up all his loose ends, pack any belongings he wanted to take with him, and move back to Trinity Lakes with her.

He squeezed her hand as the plane lifted off. "Are you ready for another adventure, my real-life Princess Jasmine?"

Violet laughed. "Stop. I'm not a princess."

"You are to me. Walked right out of my Disney dreams into real life."

"You are too much."

Nick laughed, then sobered. "Really, though. I see how the Lord orchestrated everything, to bring the best out of what seemed impossible." His thumb brushed over her fingers, sending a little thrill up her arm.

"You know, it really was crazy—you traveling to the other side of the world because you thought I was the one for you after one day."

"The best, craziest thing I ever did."

"I'm so glad you did. And yes, I see the Lord's hand in it, too."

"Hmph." He looked at her tenderly. "Let's promise now to always seek His path together, no matter what circumstances look like."

"Absolutely." She smiled back at him. "I wouldn't have it any other way."

He lifted her hand to his lips and kissed her fingers. "I love you, Violet."

Violet leaned her head on his shoulder. "I love you, too." Like he said, this would be an adventure. An adventure of a lifetime.

THE END

Enjoyed this Trinity Lakes Romance?

Then check out the next in the series, *Yesterday, Now and Always* by Sara Beth Williams.

A NOTE FROM THE AUTHOR

AUTHOR'S NOTE

Thank you for reading *Blue Skies Dreaming*. It was an honor to be included in the Trinity Lakes Series alongside some of my favorite authors. It was a step outside my usual genre of historical romance, but I loved every minute of it.

If you enjoyed this story, would you mind taking the time to put a review on the site where you purchased it, or on the Goodreads website? All reviews are helpful for authors to widen their reader base, and your support is always appreciated.

Thank you again.

Until next time,

Amanda.

Check out the other books in the Trinity Lakes series:

Never Find Another You - Narelle Atkins

The Ocean Between Us - Meredith Resce

I'll Always Choose You - Lisa Renee

Always By My Side - Iola Goulton

Where Our Hearts Lie - Jenny Glazebrook

No Matter How Far - Sara Beth Williams

Over the Rainbow - Meredith Resce

Tangled Up in Love - Carolyn Miller

In Truth and Love - Jenny Glazebrook

Blue Skies Dreaming - Amanda Deed

Yesterday, Now and Always - Sara Beth Williams

Right in Front of You - Jessica Wakefield

Always in My Heart - Iola Goulton

Only You Can Love Me - Carolyn Miller

ABOUT THE AUTHOR

Amanda Deed is an award-winning author residing in Melbourne with her husband, her grown-up children, and several birds. Outside of her family, her life revolves around words, numbers (writing and accounting) and a healthy splash of music.

Her first novel, *The Game,* won the 2010 CALEB Prize for Fiction, and she has since had several novels final in the same prize. Amanda loves to write novels that explore her faith, Australian history, and romance.

For more information, and to subscribe to her newsletter, go to
www.amandadeed.com.
She can also be found at:
www.facebook.com/AmandaDeedAuthor
www.instagram.com/ajdeed

Jackson's Creek Trilogy:

Ellenvale Gold

Black Forest Redemption

Henry's Run

Fractured Fairy Tales:

Unnoticed

Unhinged

The Captive's Song

Standalone titles:

The Game

The Greenfield Legacy

www.ingramcontent.com/pod-product-compliance
Lightning Source LLC
Chambersburg PA
CBHW030420120726
47904CB00007B/2360